The Doorbell Rang

The Doorbell Rang

A NERO WOLFE NOVEL

Rex Stout

New York · The Viking Press

The Doorbell Rang

1

Since it was the deciding factor, I might as well begin by describing it. It was a pink slip of paper three inches wide and seven inches long, and it told the First National City Bank to pay to the order of Nero Wolfe one hundred thousand and 00/100 dollars. Signed, Rachel Bruner. It was there on Wolfe's desk, where Mrs. Bruner had put it. After doing so, she had returned to the red leather chair.

She had been there half an hour, having arrived a few minutes after six o'clock. Since her secretary had phoned for an appointment only three hours earlier there hadn't been much time to check on her, but more than enough for the widow who had inherited the residual estate of Lloyd Bruner. At least eight of the several dozen buildings Bruner had left to her were more than twelve stories high, and one of them could be seen from anywhere within eye range—north, east, south, or west. All that had been necessary, really, was to ring Lon Cohen at the *Gazette* to ask if there was any news not fit to print about anyone named Bruner, but I made a couple of other calls, to a vice-president of our bank and to Nathaniel Parker, the lawyer. I got nothing, except at one point the vice-president said, "Oh . . . a funny thing . . ." and stopped.

I asked what.

Pause. "Nothing, really. Mr. Abernathy, our president, got a book from her. . . ."

"What kind of a book?"

"It—I forget. If you will excuse me, Mr. Goodwin, I'm rather busy."

So all I had on her, as I answered the doorbell in the old brownstone on West Thirty-fifth Street and let her in, and ushered her to the office, was that she had sent a man a book. After she was in the red leather chair I put her coat, which was at least a match for a sable number for which a friend of mine had paid eighteen grand, on the couch, sat at my desk, and took her in. She was a little too short and too much filled out to be rated elegant, even if her tan woolen dress was a Dior, and her face was too round, but there was nothing wrong with the brown-black eyes she aimed at Wolfe as she asked him if she needed to tell him who she was.

He was regarding her without enthusiasm. The trouble was, a new year had just started, and it seemed likely that he was going to have to go to work. In a November or December, when he was already in a tax bracket that would take three-quarters—more, formerly —of any additional income, turning down jobs was practically automatic, but January was different, and this was the fifth of January, and this woman was stacked. He didn't like it. "Mr. Goodwin named you," he said coldly, "and I read newspapers."

She nodded. "I know you do. I know a great deal about you, that's why I'm here. I want you to do something that perhaps no other man alive could do. You read books too. Have you read one entitled *The FBI Nobody Knows?*"

"Yes."

"Then I don't need to tell you about it. Did it impress you?"

"Yes."

"Favorably?"

"Yes."

"My goodness, you're curt."

"I answered your questions, madam."

"I know you did. I can be curt too. That book impressed *me*. It impressed me so strongly that I bought ten thousand copies of it and sent them to people all over the country."

"Indeed." Wolfe's brow was up an eighth of an inch.

"Yes. I sent them to the members of the cabinet, the Supreme Court justices, governors of all the states, all senators and representatives, members of state legislatures, publishers of newspapers and magazines, and editors, heads of corporations and banks, network executives and broadcasters, columnists, district attorneys, educators, and others—oh yes, chiefs of police. Do I need to explain why I did that?"

"Not to me."

There was a flash in the brown-black eyes. "I don't like your tone. I want you to do something, and I'll pay you the limit and beyond the limit, there is no limit, but there's no point in going on unless— You said that book impressed you favorably. Do you mean you agree with the author's opinion of the FBI?"

"With some minor qualifications, yes."

"And of J. Edgar Hoover?"

"Yes."

"Then it won't surprise you to hear that I am being followed day and night. I believe 'tailed' is the word. So is my son, and my daughter, and my secretary, and my brother. My telephones are tapped, and my son thinks his is—he's married and has an apartment. Some of the employees at the Bruner Corporation have been questioned. It occupies two floors of the Bruner Building and there are more than a hundred employees. Does that surprise you?"

"No." Wolfe grunted. "Did you send letters with the books?"

"Not letters. My personal card with a brief message."

"Then *you* shouldn't be surprised."

"Well, I am. I was. I'm not just a congressman, or someone like an editor or a broadcaster or a college professor, with a job I can't afford to lose. Does that megalomaniac think he can hurt *me?*"

"Pfui. He *is* hurting you."

"No. He's merely annoying me. Some of my associates and personal friends are being questioned—discreetly, of course, careful excuses, of course. It started about two weeks ago. I think my phones were tapped about ten days ago. My lawyers say there is probably no way to stop it, but they are considering it. They are one of the biggest and best firms in New York, and even *they*

are afraid of the FBI! They disapprove; they say it was
'ill-advised' and 'quixotic,' my sending the books. I
don't care what they say. When I read that book I was
furious. I called the publishers and they sent a man to
see me, and he said they had sold less than twenty
thousand copies. In a country with nearly two hundred
million people, and twenty-six million of them had
voted for Goldwater! I thought of paying for some ads,
but decided it would be better to send the books, and
I got a forty-per-cent discount on them." She curled
her fingers over the chair arms. "Now he's annoying me
and I want him stopped. I want you to stop him."

Wolfe shook his head. "Preposterous."

She reached to the stand at her elbow for her brown
leather bag, opened it, took out a checkfold and a pen,
opened the fold on the stand, no hurry, and wrote, the
stub first, with care. Methodical. She tore the check
out, got up and put it on Wolfe's desk, and returned
to the chair. "That fifty thousand dollars," she said, "is
only a retainer. I said there would be no limit."

Wolfe didn't even give the check a glance.
"Madam," he said, "I am neither a thaumaturge nor a
dunce. If you are being followed, you were followed
here, and it will be assumed that you came to hire me.
Probably another has already arrived to start surveillance of this house; if not, it will be started the instant
there is any indication that I have been ass enough to
take the job." His head turned. "Archie. How many
agents have they in New York?"

"Oh . . ." I pursed my lips. "I don't know, maybe
two hundred. They come and go."

He went back to her. "I have one. Mr. Goodwin. I
never leave my house on business. It would—"

"You have Saul Panzer and Fred Durkin and Orrie Cather."

Ordinarily that would have touched him, her rattling off their names like that, but not then. "I wouldn't ask them to take the risk," he said. "I wouldn't expect Mr. Goodwin to take it. Anyway, it would be futile and fatuous. You say 'stop him.' You mean, I take it, compel the FBI to stop annoying you?"

"Yes."

"How?"

"I don't know."

"Nor do I." He shook his head. "No, madam. You invited it, and you have it. I don't say that I disapprove of your sending the books, but I agree with the lawyers that it was quixotic. The don endured his afflictions; so must you. They won't keep it up forever, and, as you say, you're not a congressman or a drudge with a job to lose. But don't send any more books."

She was biting her lip. "I thought you were afraid of nobody and nothing."

"Afraid? I can dodge folly without backing into fear."

"I said no other man alive could do it."

"Then you're in a box."

She got her bag and opened it, took out the check-fold and pen, wrote again, the stub first as before, stepped to his desk and picked up the first check and replaced it with the new one, and returned to the chair.

"That hundred thousand dollars," she said, "is merely a retainer. I will pay all expenses. If you succeed, your fee, determined by you, will be in addition to the retainer. If you fail, you will have the hundred thousand."

He leaned forward to reach for the check, gave it a

good look, put it down, leaned back, and closed his eyes. Knowing him, I knew what he was considering. Not the job; as he had said, it was preposterous; he was looking at the beautiful fact that with a hundred grand in the till on January fifth he would need, and would accept, no jobs at all for the rest of the winter, and the spring, and even into the summer. He could read a hundred books and propagate a thousand orchids. Paradise. A corner of his mouth twisted up; for him that was a broad grin. He was wallowing. That was okay for half a minute, a man has a right to dream, but when it got to a full minute I coughed, loud.

He opened his eyes and straightened up. "Archie? Have you a suggestion?"

So it had bit him good. It was conceivable that he might even commit himself, partially at least, and of course that wouldn't do. The best way to prevent it was to get her out of there quick.

"Not offhand," I said. "No suggestion. I have a comment. You said that if she's being tailed she was followed here, but if her phone's tapped they didn't have to bother to tail her because they heard her secretary making the appointment."

He frowned. "And this house *is* under surveillance."

"Possibly. It could be that it isn't as bad as she thinks it is. Of course she wouldn't stretch it deliberately, but—"

"I don't 'stretch' things," she cut in.

"Of course not," I told her. "But," I told Wolfe, "people who aren't used to being annoyed annoy easy. We can check the tailing part right now." I turned. "Did you come in a taxi, Mrs. Bruner?"

"No. My car and chauffeur are outside."

"Fine. I'll take you out and wait there while you leave and see what happens." I stood up. "Mr. Wolfe can let you know tomorrow what he decides." I went to the couch for the sable.

It worked. She didn't like it. She had come to hire Nero Wolfe, and she hung on for five minutes trying to clinch it, but she soon saw that she was only riling him and got up and invited her coat. She was up on Wolfe all right. Aware that he didn't like to shake hands, she didn't offer, but when I followed her out to the stoop she gave my hand a firm warm clasp, having gathered that I was going to be in on the decision. There were a couple of icy spots on the seven steps of the stoop, and I took her elbow down to the sidewalk, and the chauffeur was there at the open car door to hand her in. Before she went to it she slanted the brown-black eyes up at me and said, "Thank you, Mr. Goodwin. Of course there will be a check for you, personally."

The chauffeur didn't touch her; apparently she preferred to do it herself, so she wasn't the kind of middle-aged widow who likes to feel a grip on her arm from a big strong male. When she was in he shut the door, got in front behind the wheel, and rolled; and thirty yards to the east, toward Ninth Avenue, a car whose lights had gone on and whose engine had started slid out and forward and came on by. Two men in the front seat. I stood there in the cold January wind long enough to see it take the turn into Tenth Avenue. It was laughable, so I laughed as I mounted the stoop, but I shut it off before I entered the hall.

Wolfe was leaning back with his eyes closed, but

his mouth was tight, no curl at the corner. As I crossed
to his desk he opened the eyes to slits. I picked up the
check and inspected it. I had never seen one for an
even, round, plain hundred grand, though I had seen
bigger ones. I dropped it, went to my desk, sat,
scribbled the license number of the tail car on the
scratch pad, swung the phone around, dialed a number, and got a man, a city employee for whom I had
once done a king-size favor. When I gave him the license number he said it might take an hour, and I said
I would hold my breath.

As I hung up Wolfe's voice came. "Is that flummery?"

I swiveled. "No, sir. She is in real danger. A pair of
them were in a car down the block. They switched on
their lights as she got in, and as her Rolls turned into
Tenth Avenue they were so close behind they nearly
bumped it. An open tail, but they're overdoing it. If
the Rolls stops short they'll bang it. She's in danger."

"Grrrhh," he said.

"Yes, sir. I agree. The point is, who are they? If it's
something private, that hundred grand could be
earned maybe. Of course if it's really G-men she'll just
have to endure her afflictions, *as you said*. We'll know
in an hour or so."

He glanced at the clock on the wall. Twelve minutes
to seven. He focused on me. "Is Mr. Cohen at his
office?"

"Probably. He usually quits around seven."

"Ask him to dine with us."

That was very foxy. If I said there was no point in
it since the thing was preposterous, he would say that

I was certainly aware of the importance of maintaining good relations with Mr. Cohen, which I was, and that he personally had not seen him for more than a year, which was true.

I swiveled and got the phone and dialed.

2

At nine o'clock we were back in the office, Lon in the red leather chair and Wolfe and I at our desks, and Fritz was serving coffee and brandy. The hour and a half in the dining room across the hall had been quite sociable, what with the clam cakes with chili sauce, the beef braised in red wine, the squash with sour cream and chopped dill, the avocado with watercress and black walnut kernels, and the Liederkranz. The talk had covered the state of the Union, the state of the feminine mind, whether any cooked oyster can be fit to eat, structural linguistics, and the prices of books. It had got hot only on the feminine mind, and Lon had done that purposely to see how sharp Wolfe could get.

Lon took a sip of brandy and looked at his wristwatch. "If you don't mind," he said, "let's get at it. I

have to be somewhere at ten o'clock. I know you don't
expect me to pay for my dinner, but I also know that
ordinarily, when there's something you want to get
or give, Archie just phones or drops in, so this must be
something special. It will have to be fantastic to be as
special as this cognac."

Wolfe picked up a slip of paper that was there on
his desk, frowned at it, and put it down. I had put it
there half an hour before. My dinner had been interrupted by a phone call from the city employee with
the information I had wanted, and before returning
to the dining room I had written "FBI" on a sheet from
the scratch pad and put it on Wolfe's desk. It hadn't
improved my appetite any. If she had been wrong
about the tail it could have had great possibilities, including a fat raise for me in the form of a check for
me, personally.

Wolfe sipped coffee, put the cup down, and said, "I
have fourteen bottles left."

"My God," Lon said, and sniffed the brandy. It was
funny about him. With his slicked-back hair and his
neat little tight-skinned face he looked like nobody in
particular, but somehow he always seemed to fit, whatever he was doing—in his room on the twentieth floor
in the *Gazette* building, two doors down from the publisher's corner room, or dancing with a doll at the
Flamingo, or at the table with us in Saul Panzer's
apartment where we played poker. Or sniffing a fifty-
year-old cognac.

He took a sip. "Anything you want," he said. "Barring
nothing."

"Actually," Wolfe said, "it isn't very special. Certainly not fantastic. First a question: Do you know of

any connection, however remote, between Mrs. Lloyd Bruner and the Federal Bureau of Investigation?"

"Sure I do. Who doesn't? She sent a million people copies of Fred Cook's book, including our publisher and editor. It's the latest status symbol, and damn it, I didn't get one. Did you?"

"No. I bought mine. Do you know of any action the Bureau has taken in reprisal? This is a private and confidential conversation."

Lon smiled. "Any action they might take would also be private and confidential. You'll have to ask J. Edgar Hoover—unless you already know. Do you?"

"Yes."

Lon's chin jerked up. "The hell you do. Then the people who pay his salary should know."

Wolfe nodded. "That would be your view, naturally. You seek information in order to publish it; I seek it for my private interest. At the moment I seek it only to decide where my interest lies. I have no client and no commitment, and I should make it clear that even if I commit myself and go to work I shall probably never be able to give you any publishable information, no matter what the outcome is. If I can, I will, but I doubt it. Are we in your debt?"

"No. On balance, I'm in yours."

"Good. Then I'll draw on it. Why did Mrs. Bruner send those books?"

"I don't know." He sipped brandy and moved his lips and cheeks to spread it around before swallowing. "Presumably as a public service. I bought five copies myself and sent them to people who should read them but probably won't. A man I know gave thirty copies as Christmas presents."

"Do you know if she had any private reason for animus against the FBI?"

"No."

"Have you heard any suggestion of such an animus? Any surmise?"

"No. But evidently you have. Look, Mr. Wolfe. Strictly off the record, who wants to hire you? If I knew that, I might be able to furnish a fact or two."

Wolfe refilled his cup and put the pot down. "I may not be hired," he said. "If I am, it's quite possible that you will never know who hired me. As for facts, I know what I need. I need a list of all the cases on which FBI agents have recently worked, and are now working, in and around New York. Can you supply that?"

"Hell no." Lon smiled. "I'll be damned. I was thinking—it was incredible, but I was thinking, or rather I was asking if it was possible that Hoover wanted you to work on Mrs. Bruner. That *would* be an item. But if you— I'll be damned." His eyes narrowed. "Are *you* going to perform a public service?"

"No. Nor, it may be, a private one. I'm considering it. Do you know how I can get such a list?"

"You can't. Of course some of their jobs are public knowledge, like the jewel snatch at the Natural History Museum and the bank truck at that church in Jersey —half a million in small bills. But some of them are far from public. You read that book. Of course there's talk, there's always talk, not for print. Would that help?"

"It might, especially if it was of something questionable, possibly extralegal. Is it?"

"Certainly. It's no fun talking about something that isn't questionable." He glanced at his watch. "I have twenty minutes. If I may have another small ration of brandy, and if it is understood that this is private, and if you're headed where you seem to be, I'll be glad to chip in." He looked at me. "You'll need your notebook, Archie."

Twenty minutes later his brandy glass was empty again, I had filled five pages of my notebook, and he was gone. I won't report on the contents of the five pages because very little of it was ever used, and also because some of the people named wouldn't appreciate it. At the time, as I returned to the office after seeing Lon out, my mind was on Wolfe, not the notebook. Was he actually considering it? No. Impossible. He had merely been passing the time, and of course trying to get a rise out of me. The question was how to handle it. He would be expecting me to blow my top. So I walked in and to my desk, grinned at him, said, "That was fun," yanked the five pages from the notebook, tore them in half, and was going to tear again but he bellowed, "Stop that!"

I raised one eyebrow, something he can't do. "Sorry," I said, perfectly friendly. "A souvenir?"

"No. Please sit down."

I sat. "Have I missed something?"

"I doubt it. You seldom do. A hypothetical question: If I told you that I have decided to keep that hundred thousand dollars, what would you say?"

"What you said. Preposterous."

"That's understood. But go on."

"In full?"

"Yes."

"I would say that you should sell the house and contents and go live in a nursing home, since you're ob-

viously cracked. Unless you intend to gyp her, just sit
on it."

"No."

"Then you're cracked. You've read that book. We
couldn't even get started. The idea would be to work
it so you could say to the FBI, 'Lay off,' and make it
stick. Nuts. Merely raising a stink wouldn't do it. They
would have to be actually cornered, the whole damn
outfit. Out on a limb. All right, say we try to start. We
pick one of these affairs"—I tapped the torn sheets
from the notebook—"and make some kind of a stab at
it. From then on, whenever I left the house I'd spend
all my time ditching tails, and good ones. Everyone
connected with that affair would be pegged. Our phone
would be tapped. So would other phones—for instance, Miss Rowan's, and Saul's and Fred's and
Orrie's, whether we got them in or not. And of course
Parker's. They might or might not try a frame, probably they wouldn't have to, but if they did it would
be good. I'd have to sleep here in the office. Windows
and doors, even one with a chain bolt, are pie for them.
They could monitor our mail. I am not piling it on.
How many of those things they would do would depend, but they *can* do all of them. They have all the
gimmicks there are, including some I have never heard
of."

I crossed my legs. "We'd never get to first base. But
say we did, say we actually got a wedge started in
some kind of a crack, then they would really operate.
They have six thousand trained men, some of them as
good as they come, and three hundred million dollars
a year. I would like to borrow the dictionary to look
up a stronger word than 'preposterous.'"

I uncrossed my legs. "Also, what about her? I do not believe that she is merely being annoyed. One will get you twenty that she's scared stiff. She knows there's some dirt somewhere, if not on her then on her son or daughter or brother, or even on her dead husband, and she's afraid they'll find it. She knows they're not just riding her; they're after something that would really hurt, and that would take a lot of sting out of the book. As for the hundred grand, for her that's peanuts, and anyway she's in a tax bracket that makes it petty cash."

I crossed my legs. "That's what I would say."

Wolfe grunted. "The last part was irrelevant."

"I'm often irrelevant. It confuses people."

"You keep waving your legs around."

"That confuses them too."

"Pfui. You're fidgety, and no wonder. I thought I knew you, Archie, but this is a new facet."

"It's not new at all. It's merely horse sense."

"No. Dog sense. You are moving your legs around because your tail is between them. This is what you said, in effect: I am offered a job with the largest retainer in my experience and no limit on expenses or fee, but I should decline it. I should decline it, not because it would be difficult and perhaps impossible—I have taken many jobs that seemed impossible—but because it would give offense to a certain man and his organization and he would retaliate. I decline it because I dare not take it; I would rather submit to a threat than—"

"I didn't say that!"

"It was implicit. You are cowed. You are daunted. Not, I concede, without reason; the hands and voices of many highly placed men have been stayed by the same trepidation. Possibly mine would be too if it were merely a matter of declining or accepting a job. But I will not return that check for one hundred thousand dollars because I am afraid of a bully. My self-esteem won't let me. I suggest that you take a vacation for an indefinite period. With pay; I can afford it."

I uncrossed my legs. "Beginning now?"

"Yes." He was grim.

"These notes are in my personal code. Shall I type them?"

"No. That would implicate you. I'll see Mr. Cohen again."

I clasped my hands behind my head and eyed him. "I still say you're cracked," I said, "and I deny that my tail was between my legs, since they were crossed, and it would be a ball to step aside and see how you went at it without me, but after all the years in the swim with you it would be lowdown to let you sink alone. If I get daunted along the way I'll let you know." I picked up the torn sheets. "You want this typed?"

"No. For our discussion you will translate as required."

"Right. A suggestion. The mood you're in, do you want to declare war by phoning the client? She left her unlisted number, and of course it's tapped. Shall I get her?"

"Yes."

I got at the phone and dialed.

3

Going to the kitchen before going up to bed, around midnight, to check that Fritz had bolted the back door, I was pleased to see that batter for sour-milk buckwheat cakes was there in a bowl on the range. In that situation nice crisp toast or flaky croissants would have been inadequate. So when I descended the two flights a little after nine o'clock Wednesday morning I knew I would be properly fueled. As I entered the kitchen Fritz turned up the flame under the griddle, and I told him good morning and got my orange juice from the refrigerator. Wolfe, who breakfasts in his room from a tray taken up by Fritz, had gone up to the plant rooms on the roof for his two morning hours with the orchids; I had heard the elevator as usual. As I went to the little table by the wall where I eat breakfast I asked Fritz if there was anything stirring.

"Yes," he said, "and you are to tell me what it is."

"Oh, didn't he tell you?"

"No. He said only that the doors are to be bolted and the windows locked at all times, that I am to be—what does 'circumspect' mean?"

"It means watch your step. Say nothing to anyone on the phone that you wouldn't want to see in the paper. When you go out, do nothing that you wouldn't want to see on TV. For instance, girl friends. Stay away. Swear off. Suspect all strangers."

Fritz wouldn't, and didn't, talk while cakes were getting to just the right shade of brown. When they were before me, the first two, and the sausage, and were being buttered, he said, "I want to know, Archie, and I have a right to know. He said you would explain. *Bien.* I demand it."

I picked up the fork. "You know what the FBI is."

"But certainly. Mr. Hoover."

"That's what he thinks. On behalf of a client we're going to push his nose in. Just a routine chore, but he's touchy and will try to stop us. So futile." I put a bite of cake where it belonged.

"But he—he's a great man. Yes?"

"Sure. But I suppose you've seen pictures of him."

"Yes."

"What do you think of his nose?"

"Not good. Not exactly *épaté*, but broad. Not *bien fait.*"

"Then it should be pushed." I forked sausage.

So he was at ease when I finished and went to the office. The meals would be okay, at least for today. As I dusted the desks, tore sheets from the calendars, and opened the mail, which was mostly junk, I was considering an experiment. If I dialed a number, any num-

ber, say Parker's, I might be able to tell if we were
tapped. It would be interesting to know if they had
already reacted to the call to Mrs. Bruner. I vetoed it.
I intended to keep strictly to my instructions. Doing so,
I got my pocket notebook and another item from a
drawer of my desk, opened the safe to get the check,
went to the kitchen to tell Fritz not to expect me for
lunch and to the hall rack for my hat and coat, and
departed.

Heading east, I merely walked. It's a cinch to spot a
tail, even a good one, especially on a winter day when
a cold, gusty wind is keeping the sidewalk traffic down,
but presumably they knew where I was going, so why
bother? At the bank, on Lexington Avenue, I had the
pleasure of seeing the teller's eyes widen a little as he
gave the check a second glance. The simple pleasures
of the rich. Outside again, I turned uptown. I had two
miles to go, but it was only twenty after ten, I am a
walker, and if I had a tail it would be good for his lungs
and legs.

The four-story stone on Seventy-fourth Street between Madison and Park was at least twice as wide as
Wolfe's brownstone, but it wasn't brown. The door to
the vestibule, three steps down, was solid, but the inside one was a metal grille with glass. It was opened by
a man in black with no lips who swung it wide only
after he had my name. He led me down the hall to an
open door on the left and motioned me in.

It was an office, not large—filing cabinets, a safe, two
desks, shelves, a cluttered table. On the wall back of
the table was a blow-up of the Bruner building. My
quick glance around came to rest on a face, a face that
rated a glance, belonging to the female seated at one

of the desks. Her hazel eyes were meeting the glance.

"I'm Archie Goodwin," I said.

She nodded. "I'm Sarah Dacos. Have a seat, Mr. Goodwin." She lifted the receiver from a phone and pressed a button, in a moment told someone I was there, hung up, and told me Mrs. Bruner would be down soon. Sitting, I asked her, "How long have you been with Mrs. Bruner?"

She smiled. "I know you're a detective, Mr. Goodwin, you don't have to prove it."

I smiled back. "I have to keep in practice." She was easy to smile at. "How long?"

"Nearly three years. Do you want it exactly?"

"Later maybe. Shall I wait until Mrs. Bruner comes?"

"Not necessarily. She said you would ask me some questions."

"Then I will. What did you do before?"

"I was a stenographer at the Bruner Corporation, and then Mr. Thompson's secretary, the vice-president."

"Have you ever worked for the government? For instance, for the FBI?"

She smiled. "No. Never. I was twenty-two years old when I started with the Bruner Corporation. I'm twenty-eight now. You're not taking notes."

"In here." I touched my forehead. "What gave you the idea that the FBI is tailing you?"

"I don't *know* it's the FBI. But it must be, because nobody else would."

"How sure are you you're being tailed?"

"Oh, I'm positive. I don't keep looking behind me, nothing like that, but my hours here are irregular, I leave at different times, but when I go to the bus stop a man always comes and gets on after me, and he gets off where I do. The same man."

"Madison Avenue bus?"

"No, Fifth Avenue. I live in the Village."

"When did it start?"

"I'm not sure. The first I noticed him was the Monday after Christmas. He's there in the morning, too. And in the evening, if I go out. I didn't know it was done like that. I thought if you followed someone you didn't want her to know it."

"It depends. Sometimes you do want her to know. It's called an open tail. Can you describe the man?"

"I certainly can. He's six or seven inches taller than me, about thirty years old, maybe a little more, a long face with a square chin, a long thin nose, a small straight mouth. His eyes are a kind of greenish gray. He always has his hat on, so I don't know about his hair."

"Have you ever spoken to him?"

"Of course not."

"Have you reported it to the police?"

"No, the lawyer said not to. Mrs. Bruner's lawyer. He said that if it's the FBI they can always say it's a security check."

"So they can. And do. By the way, did you suggest sending people copies of that book to Mrs. Bruner?"

Her brow went up. It was a nice smooth brow. "Why, no. I hadn't read it. I only read it afterwards."

"After you got a tail?"

"No, after she decided to send all those copies."

"Do you know who did suggest it to her?"

"I don't know if anyone did." She smiled. "I suppose it's natural, your asking me that, since you're a detective, but to me it would seem more natural to ask her. Even if I knew someone suggested it, I don't think—"

There were footsteps in the hall, approaching, and Mrs. Bruner appeared. As she entered I arose, and so did Sarah Dacos. I moved to meet her and take the offered hand and return the greeting, and when she went to sit at the other desk I changed to another chair. She gave a pile of papers under a weight a mere glance and pushed it aside, and said to me, "I suspect that I owe you some thanks, Mr. Goodwin. More than just thanks."

I shook my head. "No, you don't. Not that it matters, since the check has been deposited, but I was against it. Now that it's a job I'm for it." I got from a pocket the item I had taken from my desk drawer and handed it to her. It was a sheet of paper on which I had typed:

Mr. Nero Wolfe
914 West 35th Street
New York City 1   January 6, 1965

Dear Sir:

Confirming our conversation of yesterday, I hereby engage you to act in my interest in the matter we discussed. I believe the Federal Bureau of Investigation is responsible for the espionage I and my family and associates are being subjected to, for the reasons I gave you, but whoever is responsible, you are to investigate it and use your best efforts to have it stopped. Whatever the outcome, the $100,000 I have given you as a retainer will not be subject to any claim by me. I will pay any expenses you incur in my behalf, and if you get the result I desire I will pay a fee to be determined by you.

(Mrs. Lloyd Bruner)

She read it twice, first skimming and then every word. She looked up. "I'm supposed to sign this?"

"Yes."

"I can't. I never sign anything my lawyer hasn't read."

"You can call him and read it to him."

"But my telephone is tapped."

"I know. It's barely possible that when they know that you are giving Nero Wolfe a free hand, no limit, they'll cool off. Tell the lawyer that. Not that they're in awe of him, they're not in awe of anybody, but they know a lot about him. As for that last sentence, the fee to be determined by him, there's a loophole. It says 'if you get the result I desire.' Obviously that will be determined by you, so you're not signing a blank check. The lawyer should agree."

She read it again, then leveled the brown-black eyes at me. "I can't do that. My lawyers don't know I went to Nero Wolfe. They wouldn't approve. No one knows but Miss Dacos."

"Then we're up a stump." I turned a palm up. "Look, Mrs. Bruner. Mr. Wolfe couldn't possibly tackle it without something in writing. What if it got so hot you wanted out, leaving him in? What if you tried to hedge on what you hired him to do and wanted the retainer back?"

"I wouldn't do that. I'm not a hedger, Mr. Goodwin."

"Good. Then go ahead and sign it."

She looked at it, at me, back at it, and at Miss Dacos. "Here, Sarah," she said, "make a copy of it."

"I have a carbon," I said, and handed it to her. By gum, she read it through. Well trained by her husband, or by the lawyers after he died. She took a pen from a stand and signed the original, and I reached for it.

"So that's why Mr. Wolfe wanted you to come this morning," she said.

I nodded. "Partly. He wanted me to ask Miss Dacos a few questions about being tailed, and I have. I saw your tail yesterday. When you left a car followed you, close, with two men in it, and I got the license number. They were FBI. They want you to know. From here on we probably won't have anything to ask you or tell you unless and until there's a break, but we might, and there should be an arrangement. Since you have read that book, you know what 'bugged' means. Do you know if this room is bugged?"

"No, I don't. Of course I've thought about it, and we have examined it several times. I'm not sure. They have to get in, don't they? Put something in it?"

"Yes. Unless electronics has come up with something that isn't being mentioned, and I doubt it. I don't want to overplay it, Mrs. Bruner, but I don't think any part of this house is a good place to talk. It's cold out, but a little fresh air will do you good. If you'll get a coat?"

She nodded. "You see, Mr. Goodwin. *In my own house.* All right." She got up. "Wait here." She went.

Sarah Dacos was smiling at me. "You could have gone upstairs," she said. "I can't hear through walls or even through keyholes."

"No?" I looked her up and down, glad to have an excuse. She was very lookable. "You may be wired for sound, and there would be only one way to make sure, and you wouldn't enjoy it."

The hazel eyes laughed. "How do you know I wouldn't?"

"My knowledge of human nature. You're the squeamish type. You haven't walked up to your tail and said what's your name and what do you want."

"Why, do you think I should?"

"No. But you haven't. May I ask, do you dance?"

"Sometimes."

"I'd know more about you if you danced with me. I don't mean about the possibility that you're playing with the FBI. If they had you, right here in the house, they wouldn't be dogging her and the whole family. The only reason I—"

The client showed at the door. I hadn't heard her footsteps. That was bad. Miss Dacos was attractive, but not enough to keep me from hearing footsteps, even though I was talking. That could only mean that my opinion of the job wouldn't let me get fully on it, all of me, and that wouldn't do. As I went and followed the client to the front my jaw was set. The man in black opened the door, and I got the vestibule door, and we were out in the January wind. We headed east, toward Park Avenue, and stopped at the corner.

"We can talk better standing," I said. "First, our getting you in a hurry if we have to. There's absolutely no telling what's going to happen. It's even possible that Mr. Wolfe and I will have to leave his house and hole up somewhere. If you get a message, by phone or otherwise, no matter how, that the pizza is sour, go at once to the Churchill Hotel and find a man named William Coffey. He's a house dick there—an assistant security officer. You can do that openly. He'll have something for you, either to tell you or give you. Pizza is sour. Churchill Hotel, William Coffey. Remember it. Don't write it down."

"I won't." She was frowning. "I suppose you're sure you can trust him?"

"Yes. If you knew Mr. Wolfe better, and me, you wouldn't ask that. Have you got it?"

"Yes." She pulled the collar of her coat, not the sable, something else, closer.

"Okay. Now your getting us if you have to, for something not to be spilled. Go to a phone booth and ring Mr. Wolfe's number and tell whoever answers that Fido is sick, just that, and hang up. Wait two hours and go to the Churchill and William Coffey. Of course this is just for something they are not to know. For anything they have done or already know about, just ring us. Fido is sick."

She was still frowning. "But they'll know about William Coffey after the first time if I go to him openly."

"We may use him only once. Leave that to us. Actually, Mrs. Bruner, you're more or less out of it now, the operation. We'll be working for you, but not on you or about you. We probably won't need to make contact with you at all. All this is just a precaution in case. But there's something we ought to know now. You said you came to Mr. Wolfe and gave him that six-figure check merely because you're being annoyed. Of course you're a very wealthy woman, but that's hard to believe. It's a good guess that there's something buried somewhere—about you or yours—that you don't want dug up, and you're afraid they will. If that's so we ought to know it—not what it is, but how urgent it is. Are they getting close?"

A gust of wind slapped her and she bent her head and hunched a shoulder. "No," she said, but the wind swept it away and she said it louder. "No."

"But of course they might."

Her eyes were focused on me, but the wind made it a squint. "We won't discuss that, Mr. Goodwin," she said. "I suppose every family has its . . . something. Perhaps I didn't consider that risk enough when I sent those books, but I did it, and I don't regret it. They're not 'getting close' to anything, as far as I know. Not yet."

"That's all you want to say about it?"

"Yes."

"Okay. If and when you want to say more you know what to do. What is sour?"

"The pizza."

"Who is sick?"

"Fido."

"What's his name?"

"William Coffey. At the Churchill."

"Good enough. You'd better get back in, your ears are red. I'll probably see you again some day, but God knows when."

She touched my arm. "What are you going to do?"

"Look around. Buzz. Pry."

She was going to say something, decided not to, and turned and went. I stood until she reached her door and went in, then headed west. There was no point in casing areaways or windows, but I gave the parked cars a glance as I passed, and a little this side of Madison Avenue there was one with two men in the front seat. I stopped. They weren't looking at me, the way they are trained not to look in Washington. I backed up a couple of steps, got my notebook out, and jotted down the license number. If they wanted it open, why not? They still not-looked, and I went on.

Turning down Madison, I didn't bother about spotting a tail, since I had made arrangements on the phone, from a booth the night before, with a hackie I knew, Al Goller. My watch said 11:35, so I had plenty of time and stopped here and there on the way to look in shop windows. At the corner of Sixty-fifth Street I entered a drugstore with a lunch counter, mounted a stool near the front, and ordered a corned-beef sandwich on rye and a glass of milk. There is never any corned beef or rye bread at Wolfe's table. When that was down I requested a piece of apple pie and coffee. At 12:27 I finished the second cup and twisted around on the stool to look through the window. At 12:31 a brown and yellow taxi rolled to a stop out in front, and I moved, fast—almost not fast enough because a woman was making for the door. I beat her to it and climbed in, and Al pushed the OFF DUTY sign up, and the flag, and we were off.

"Not the cops, I hope," Al said over his shoulder.

"Nope," I said. "Arabs on camels. Turn corners awhile. A very slim chance, but I need to be loose. Excuse my back." I turned around on the seat to watch the rear. Six turns and ten minutes later there was no question about being clear and I told him First Avenue and Thirty-sixth Street. There I gave him a sawbuck and told him to sit twenty minutes and then shove off if I didn't show. A finif would have been enough, but the client could afford it, and we would probably need Al again. Again and again. I walked a block and a half south, entered a building that hadn't been there three years back, consulted the directory on the wall of the lobby, learned that Evers Electronics, Inc., was on the eighth floor, and took the elevator.

They had the whole floor; the receptionist's desk was right there when I left the elevator, and at it was not the regulation female but a broad-shouldered husky with a square chin and unfriendly eyes. I crossed to him and said, "Mr. Adrian Evers, please. My name is Archie Goodwin."

He didn't believe it. He wouldn't have believed it if I had said today is January sixth. He asked, "You have an appointment?"

"No. I work for Nero Wolfe, the private investigator. I have some information for Mr. Evers."

He didn't believe that either. "You say Nero Wolfe?"

"I do. Got a Bible?"

Not bothering to resent it, he got at a phone and did some talking and listening, hung up, told me, "Wait here," and cocked his head at me. He was probably deciding how much of a job it would be to take me. To show him I wasn't fazed I turned my back and went to inspect a picture on the wall, a photograph of a sprawling two-story building with the inscription EVERS ELECTRONICS DAYTON PLANT. I had about finished counting the windows when a door opened to admit a woman who pronounced my name and told me to come, and I followed her down a hall and around a corner to a door that had MR. EVERS on it. She opened it and I entered, but she didn't.

He was at a desk between two windows, taking a bite from a sandwich. Two steps in I stopped and said, "But I don't want to butt in on your lunch."

He chewed the bite, sizing me up through his rimless cheaters. His neat little face was the kind that doesn't register unless you make a point of it. When the bite was down he took a sip of coffee from a paper cup and said, "Someone always butts in. What's this about Nero Wolfe and information? What kind of information?" He took a bite of the sandwich, lox on white toast.

I went to a chair near the end of his desk and sat. "You may already have it," I said. "It's in connection with a government contract."

He chewed and swallowed and asked, "Is Nero Wolfe working for the government?"

"No. He's working for a private client. The client is interested in the fact that after a security check of an officer of your company the government has canceled a contract, or is about to. That's a matter of public interest, and—"

"Who is the client?"

"I can't name him. It's confidential, and—"

"Is it anyone connected with this company?"

"No. Not in any way. As I was saying, Mr. Evers, the public interest is involved, you realize that. If the right to make security checks is being abused so that the personal or property rights of citizens are being violated, that isn't just a private matter. Mr. Wolfe's client is concerned with that aspect of it. Anything you tell me will be strictly confidential and will be used only with your permission. Naturally you don't want to lose your contract, we understand it's a big one, but also as a citizen you don't want to see any injustice done. From the standpoint of Mr. Wolfe's client, that's the issue."

He had put the sandwich down, what was left of it, and was eying me. "You said you had information. What?"

"Well, we thought it possible that you didn't know that the contract is going to be canceled."

"A hundred people know that. What else?"

"Apparently the reason for the cancelation is that the security check on your senior vice-president uncovered certain facts about his personal life. That raises two questions: how accurate are the so-called facts, and do they actually make him or your company a security risk? Is he, and are you, getting a raw deal?"

"What else?"

"That's it. I should think that's enough, Mr. Evers. If you don't want to discuss it with me, discuss it with Mr. Wolfe himself. If you don't know about his standing and reputation, check on it. He told me to make it clear that if you get any benefit from anything he does he would expect no payment of any kind. He isn't looking for a client; he has one."

He was frowning at me. "I don't get it. The client —is it a newspaper?"

"No."

"A magazine? *Time?*"

"No." I decided to stretch my instructions a little. "I can only tell you it's a private citizen who thinks the FBI is getting too big for its britches."

"I don't believe it. And I damn well don't like it." He pushed a button on a slab. "Are *you* FBI?"

I said no and was going on, but the door opened and a woman was there, the one who had led me in, and Evers snapped at her, "See this man out, Miss Bailey. Into the elevator."

I objected. I said that if he discussed it with Nero Wolfe the worst that could happen would be losing his contract, and evidently it was lost anyway, and if there was any chance of saving it— But the look on his face showed me it was no good, as he reached for the slab to push another button. No sale and no hope for one. I got up and walked out, with the woman tagging, and found, out in the ante-room, that it just wasn't my day. As I entered, the elevator door opened and a man came out, and it wasn't a stranger. Working on a case about a year ago I had had dealings with a G-man named Morrison, and there he was. Our eyes met, and then we met. As he offered a hand he spoke. "Well, well. Is Nero Wolfe using electronics now?"

I gave him a friendly grip and a grin. "Oh," I said, "we try to keep up. We're going to bug a certain building on Sixty-ninth Street." I stepped to the elevator and pushed the button. "I'm getting the latest angles."

He laughed to be polite and said he guessed they'd have to do all their talking in code. The elevator door opened, and I entered and the door slid shut. It certainly wasn't my day. Not that it mattered much, since I had got nowhere with Evers, but it's always bad to have the breaks going wrong, and God knows if we ever needed the breaks we did then. I was walking on hard pavement, not air, as I emerged to the sidewalk and turned uptown.

It had been more than twenty minutes, and Al had gone. There are plenty of taxis on First Avenue at that hour, and I flagged one and gave the hackie an address.

4

At a quarter to eleven that Wednesday night, pessimistic and pooped, I mounted the stoop of the old brownstone and pushed the button. With the chain bolt on I had to be let in. When Fritz came he asked if I wanted some warmed-up curried duck, and I growled the no. I shed my hat and coat and went to the office, and there was the oversized genius at his desk, in the chair made to order for his seventh of a ton, with a bottle of beer and a glass on the tray, comfortably reading his current book, *The Treasure of Our Tongue*, by Lincoln Barnett. I went to my desk and whirled my chair and sat. He would look up when he finished a paragraph.

He did. He even inserted his bookmark, a thin strip of gold given him years before by a client who couldn't afford it, and put the book down. "You have dined, of course," he said.

"Dined, no." I crossed my legs. "Excuse me for waving my legs around. I ate something greasy, I forget what, in a dump in the Bronx. It has been—"

"Fritz will warm the duck, and—"

"No he won't. I told him not to. It has been by far the lousiest day I have ever had and I'll finish it up right. I'll report in full and go to bed tasting grease. First, the—"

"Confound it, you must eat!"

"I say no. First, the client."

I gave it to him verbatim, and the action, including the two men in the parked car of which I had the license number. At the end I added some opinions: that (a) it would be wasting a dime to bother to check the license number, (b) Sarah Dacos could probably be crossed off, or at least filed for future reference, and (c) whatever dirt there might be under cover in the Bruner family, the lid was still on as far as the client knew. When I got up to hand him the paper Mrs. Bruner had signed he merely glanced at it and said to put it in the safe.

I also gave him the Evers thing verbatim, of course including Morrison. My only opinion on that was that I hadn't handled it right, that I should have told him we had secret information he didn't have and couldn't get, and we might be able to put on pressure that would save his contract, and if we did we would expect to be paid. Of course it would have been risky, but it might have opened him up. Wolfe shook his head and said it would have made us too vulnerable. I rose and circled around his desk to the stand that held the dictionary, opened it and found what I wanted, and returned to my chair.

"Capable of being wounded," I said. "Liable to attack or injury. That's what 'vulnerable' means. It would be quite a trick to get any more vulnerable than we are now. But to finish the day. It took me all afternoon to run down Ernst Muller, who is charged with conspiring to transport stolen property across state lines and is out on bail, and he was even worse than Evers. He had the idea of slugging me, and he wasn't alone, so I had to react, and I may have broken his arm. Then—"

"Were you hurt?"

"Only my feelings. Then, after eating the grease, I set out for Julia Fenster, who was or wasn't framed for espionage and was tried and acquitted, and that's how I spent the evening, all of it, trying to find her. I finally found her brother, but not her, and he's a fish. No man ever got less out of a day. It's a record. And those were the three we picked as the best prospects. I can't wait to see the program you've planned for tomorrow. I'll put it under my pillow."

"It's partly your stomach," he said. "If not the duck, then an omelet."

"No."

"Caviar. There's a fresh pound."

"You know damn well I love caviar. I wouldn't insult it."

He poured beer, waited until the foam was down to half an inch, drank, licked his lips, and regarded me. "Archie. Are you trying to pester me into returning that retainer?"

"No. I know I couldn't."

"Then you're twaddling. You're quite aware that we have undertaken a job which, considered logically, is preposterous. We have both said so. It's extremely un-

likely that any of the suggestions Mr. Cohen gave us
will give us a start, but it's conceivable that one might.
There's some hit-or-miss in every operation, but this one
is all hit-or-miss. We are at the mercy of the vicissitudes
of fortune; we can only invite, not command. I have no
program for tomorrow; it depended on today. You don't
know that today was bootless. Some prick may have
stirred someone to action. Or tomorrow it may, or next
week. You're tired and hungry. Confound it, eat something!"

I shook my head. "What about tomorrow?"

"We'll consider that in the morning. Not tonight." He
picked up his book.

I left my chair, gave it a kick, got the paper from my
desk and put it in the safe, and went to the kitchen and
poured a glass of milk. Fritz had gone down to bed.
Realizing that what would be an insult to caviar would
also be an insult to milk, I poured it back in the carton,
got another glass and the bottle of Old Sandy bourbon,
poured three fingers, and took a healthy swig. That took
care of the grease all right, and after going to see that
the back door was bolted I finished the bourbon, rinsed
the glasses, went and mounted the two flights to my
room, and changed into pajamas and slippers.

I considered taking my electric blanket but vetoed
it. In a pinch a man must expect hardship. From my
bed I took only the pillow, and got sheets and blankets
from the closet in the hall. With my arms loaded I
descended, went to the office, removed the cushions
from the couch, and spread the sheets. As I was un-
folding a blanket Wolfe's voice came.

"I question the need for that."

"I don't." I spread the blanket, and the other one,

and turned. "You've read that book. They can move fast if and when. With some of the stuff in the files they could have a picnic—and the safe."

"Bah. You're stretching it. Blow open a safe in an occupied house?"

"They wouldn't have to, that antique. You ought to get some books on electronics." I tucked the blankets in at the foot.

He pushed his chair back, levered himself up, said good night, and went, taking *The Treasure of Our Tongue.*

Thursday morning there was an off chance that when Fritz came down from delivering the breakfast tray he would bring word for me to go up for a briefing, but he didn't. So, since Wolfe wouldn't be down from the plant rooms until eleven, I took my time with the routine, and it was going on ten when everything was under control—the bedding back upstairs, breakfast inside me, the *Times* looked at, the mail opened and under a paperweight on Wolfe's desk, and Fritz explained to. Explained to, but not at ease. He had a vivid memory, as we all did, of the night that machine guns on a roof across the street had strafed the plant rooms, shattering hundreds of panes of glass and ruining thousands of orchids, and his idea was that I was sleeping in the office because my room faced Thirty-fifth Street and there was going to be a repeat performance. I explained that I was a guard, not a refugee, but he didn't believe it and said so.

In the office, after opening the mail, all I had to pass was time. There was a phone call for Fritz from a fish man, and I listened in, but got no sign that the line was tapped, though of course it was. Hooray for the technicians. Modern science was fixing it so that anybody can do anything but nobody can know what the hell is going on. I got my notebook from a drawer and went through the dope Lon Cohen had given us, considering the possibilities. There were fourteen items altogether, and at least five of them were obviously hopeless. Of the other nine we had made a stab at three and got nothing. That left six, and I sized them up, one by one. I decided that the most promising one, or anyway the least unpromising, concerned a woman who had been fired from a job in the State Department and got it back, and was reaching for the Washington phone book to see if she was listed when the doorbell rang.

Going to the hall for a look through the one-way glass in the front door, I was expecting to see a stranger, and maybe two. The direct approach. Or possibly Morrison. But there was a well-known face and figure on the stoop—Dr. Vollmer, whose office is in a house he owns down the block. I went and opened the door and greeted him, and he entered, along with a lot of fresh icy air. Turning from shutting the door, I told him if he was drumming up trade he'd have to try next door, and put out a hand for his hat.

He kept it on. "I've got too much trade as it is, Archie. Everybody's sick. But I've got a message for you, just now on the phone. A man, no name. He said to give it to you personally. You're to be at the Westside Hotel, Room Two-fourteen, on Twenty-third Street, at eleven-thirty or as soon thereafter as you can make it, and you must be sure you're loose."

My brows were up. "Quite a message."

"That's what I thought. He said you would tell me to keep it under my hat."

"Okay, I tell you. That's why you're keeping it on." I looked at my wrist: 10:47. "What else did he say?"

"That's all, just the message, after he asked if I would come and tell you personally."

"Room Two-fourteen, Westside Hotel."

"That's right."

"What kind of a voice?"

"No particular kind, nothing distinctive, neither high nor low. Just a normal man's voice."

"All right, Doc, many thanks. We need another favor if you can spare it. We're on an operation that's a little tricky, and you were probably seen. It's possible that someone will want to know why you called. If anybody asks, you might—"

"I'll say you phoned and asked me to come and look at your throat."

"No. Wrong twice. He'll know there's nothing wrong with my throat, and he'll know I didn't phone. Our line is tapped. The trouble is that if someone gets the notion that we get confidential messages through you, your line will be tapped."

"My God. But that's illegal!"

"That makes it more fun. If anybody asks, you might be indignant and say it's none of his damned business, or you might be obliging and say you came to take Fritz's blood pressure—no, you haven't got the gadget. You came—"

"I came to get his recipe for *escargots bourguignonne*. I like that better, nonprofessional." He moved to the door. "My word, Archie, it certainly *is* tricky."

I agreed and thanked him again, and he said to give his regards to Wolfe. When I closed the door after him I didn't bother to slide the bolt since I would soon be leaving. I went to the kitchen and told Fritz he had just given the recipe for *escargots bourguignonne* to Dr. Vollmer, and then to the office and buzzed the plant rooms on the house phone. I refused to believe they could tap a house phone. Wolfe answered, and I told him. He grunted and asked, "Have you any notion?"

"Not the vaguest. Not the FBI. Why would they? It could be that quote some prick may have stirred someone end of quote. Evers or Miss Fenster or even Muller. Any instructions?"

He said pfui and hung up, and I admit I had asked for it.

There would be the problem of spotting a tail and shaking it, and that can take time, so I would have to get help if I wanted to be punctual for the appointment. Also I should be prepared for the remote possibility that Ernst Muller was sensitive about having his arm twisted and was intending to return the compliment, so I got the shoulder holster from the drawer and put it on, and the Marley .38, and loaded it. But another kind of ammunition might be needed, and I opened the safe and got a grand in used tens and twenties from the cash reserve. Of course there were other conceivables, such as that I was going to have my picture taken in a room with a naked female or a corpse or God knew what, but I would have to dive off of that bridge when I came to it.

It was one minute to eleven when I left the house. With no glance around, I walked to the drugstore at the corner of Ninth Avenue, entered, went to the phone booth, and dialed the number of the garage on Tenth Avenue which houses the Heron sedan that Wolfe owns and I drive. Tom Halloran, who had been there for ten years, didn't answer, but after a wait I got him and explained the program, and he said he would be ready in five minutes. Thinking it would be better to give him ten, I looked over the rack of paperbacks awhile before leaving. Heading back on Thirtyfifth Street, I went on past the brownstone, turned right at Tenth Avenue, entered the garage office, went on through, and crossed to a Ford sedan standing there with the engine running. Tom was in front behind the wheel. I climbed in the back, took my hat off and curled up on the floor, clear down, and the car moved.

There may be leg room in that Ford model, but there's not body room for a six-footer who is not an expert contortionist, and I suffered. After five minutes of it I began to suspect that Tom was jerking to stops and around corners just to see how tough I was, but I was stuck, in more ways than one. My ribs were about to give and my legs were going numb when he stopped for the sixth time and his voice came. "All right, pal. All clear."

"Damn it, get a crowbar."

He laughed. I worked my head and shoulders up, got a grip on the rim of the seat back, somehow made it, and put my hat on. We were at Twenty-third Street and Ninth Avenue. "How sure are you?" I asked him.

"Posilutely. Not a chance."

"Wonderful. But the next time use an ambulance. You'll find a piece of my ear in the corner. Keep it to remember me by."

I got out. He asked if there was anything more, and I said no and I would thank him later, and he rolled.

The Westside Hotel, in the middle of the block, was not exactly a dump, though many people would call it

that. Evidently it was still in the black, since it had put
on a new front and redone the lobby a couple of years
back. Entering and ignoring everybody and everything,
including a bald bellhop, I went to the do-it-yourself
elevator, pushed the button, and was lifted. As I
emerged and went to the nearest door to look at the
number I noticed that my hand had slipped inside my
coat to touch the Marley, and grinned at myself. If it
was J. Edgar Hoover waiting for me, apparently he had
better behave or he might get plugged. At Room 214,
halfway down the hall on the left, the door was closed.
My watch said 11:33. I knocked, and heard footsteps,
and the door opened; and I stood and gawked. I was
looking at the round red face and burly figure of Inspector Cramer of Homicide South.

"Right on time," he growled. "Come in." He side-
stepped, and I crossed the sill.

My eyes have been trained so long to notice things
that they took in the room automatically—the double
bed, dresser with a mirror, two chairs, table with a desk
pad that needed changing, open door to a bathroom—
while my mind adjusted to the shock. Then, as I put
my coat and hat on the bed, I got another shock: one
of the chairs, the one without arms, was near the table,
and on the table was a carton of milk and a glass. By
God, he had bought it and brought it for his guest. I
don't blame you if you don't believe it. I didn't, but
there it was.

He went to the other chair, the one with arms, sat,
and asked, "Are you loose?"

"Sure. I always obey instructions."

"Sit down."

I went to the other chair. He leveled his gray eyes at me. "Is Wolfe's phone tapped?"

My eyes were meeting his. "Look," I said, "you know damn well how it is. If I had listed a hundred names of people who might be here, yours wouldn't have been on it. Is this carton of milk for me?"

"Yes."

"Then you're off your hinges. You are not the Inspector Cramer I know so well, and I don't know what I'm up against. Why do you want to know if our phone is tapped?"

"Because I don't like to make things more complicated than they are already. I like things simple. I'd like to know if I could just have called you and asked you to come here."

"Oh. Sure you could, but if you had I would have suggested that it might be better if we went for a ride."

He nodded. "All right. I want to know, Goodwin. I know Wolfe has tangled with the FBI, and I want the picture. All of it. If it takes all day."

I shook my head. "That's out of bounds and you know it."

He exploded. "Goddammit, *this* is out of bounds! My being here! My getting you here! I thought you had some sense! Don't you realize what I'm doing?"

"No. I haven't the slightest idea what you're doing."

"Then I'll tell you. I know you pretty well, Goodwin. I know you and Wolfe cut corners, I ought to, but I also know what your limits are. So here, just you and me, I'll tell you. About two hours ago the Commissioner called me. He had had a call from Jim Perazzo—do you know who Jim Perazzo is?"

"Yeah, I happen to. Licensing Services, State Department, State of New York. Two-seventy Broadway."

"You would. I won't string it out. The FBI wants Perazzo to take Wolfe's license, and yours. Perazzo wants the Commissioner to give him whatever we've got on you. The Commissioner knows that for years I have had —uh—contacts with you, and he wants a full report, in writing. You know what reports are, it depends on who's writing them. Before I write this one I want to know what Wolfe has done or is doing to get the FBI on his neck. I want the whole picture."

When you are shown something that needs a good look it helps to have your hands doing something, like lighting a cigarette, but I don't smoke, or blowing your nose. I picked up the carton of milk, pried the flap open, and poured, carefully. One thing was obvious. He could have either phoned me to come to his office, or have come to Wolfe's house, but he hadn't because he suspected that our line was tapped and the house was watched. Therefore he didn't want the FBI to know that he was making contact, and he had gone to a lot of trouble to make it. He was telling me about the FBI and Perazzo and the Commissioner, which was ridiculous for a police inspector talking to a private detective. Therefore he didn't want us to lose our licenses, and therefore something was biting him, and it was desirable to find out what it was. In such a situation, before spilling it, especially to a cop, I should ring Wolfe and put it up to him, but that was out. My standing instructions were that in any emergency I was to use my intelligence guided by experience.

I did so. I sipped some milk, put the glass down, and said, "If you can break a rule so can I. It's like this."

I gave him the whole crop—the talk with Mrs. Bruner, the hundred-grand retainer, the evening with Lon Cohen, my talk with Mrs. Bruner and Sarah Dacos, my day on Evers Electronics and Ernst Muller and Julia Fenster, my sleeping on the couch in the office. I didn't report it all verbatim, but I covered all the points and answered questions along the way. By the time I finished the milk glass was empty and he had a cigar between his teeth. He doesn't smoke cigars, he merely mangles them.

He removed the cigar and said, "So the hundred grand is his, no matter what happens."

I nodded. "And a check for me, personally. Didn't I mention that?"

"You did. I'm not surprised at Wolfe. With his ego, there's no one and nothing he wouldn't take on if you paid him. But I'm surprised at you. You know damn well the FBI can't be bucked. Not even by the White House. And you're hopping around pecking at people's scabs. You're asking for it and you'll get it. You're off *your* hinges."

I poured milk. "You're absolutely right," I said. "From any angle, you're dead right. An hour ago I would have said amen. But you know, I feel different about it now. Did I mention something Mr. Wolfe said last night? He said some sting may have stirred someone to action. All right, they were stung into needling Perazzo, and he was stung into calling the Commissioner, and he was stung into calling you, and you were stung into getting me here without company and treating me to a quart of milk, which is completely incredible. If one incredible thing can happen, so can another one. Will you answer a question?"

"Ask it."

"You don't exactly love Nero Wolfe, and you certainly don't love me. Why do you want to make a report to the Commissioner that will make it tough to take our licenses?"

"I haven't said I do."

"Nuts." I tapped the milk carton. "This says it. Getting me here the way you did says it. Why?"

He left the chair and moved. He tiptoed to the door, smooth and silent considering his age and bulk, jerked the door open, and stuck his head out. Evidently he wasn't as sure he was loose as I was that I was. He shut the door and went to the bathroom, and I heard water spurting from a faucet, and in a minute he came with a glass of water. He drank it, in no hurry, put the glass on the table, sat, and narrowed his eyes at me.

"I've been a cop for thirty-six years," he said, "and this is the first time I've ever passed the buck to an outsider."

I had my eyes smile a little. "I'm flattered. Or Mr. Wolfe is."

"Balls. He wouldn't know flattery if it had labels pasted all over it, and neither would you. Goodwin, I'm going to tell you something that's for you and Wolfe, and that's *all*. No Lon Cohen or Saul Panzer or Lily Rowan. Is that understood?"

"I don't know why you drag in Miss Rowan, she's merely a personal friend. And there's no point in telling me something if we can't use it."

"You'll use it all right. But it did *not* come from me. Never, to anybody."

"Okay. Mr. Wolfe isn't here to cinch it by giving you

his word of honor, so I'll do it for him. For us. Our word of honor."

"That'll have to do. You won't have to take notes, with your tape-recorder memory. Does the name Morris Althaus mean anything to you?" He spelled it.

I nodded. "I read the papers. One that you haven't cracked. Shot. In the chest. Late November. No gun."

"Friday night, November twentieth. The body was found the next morning by a cleaning woman. Died between eight p.m. Friday and three a.m. Saturday. One shot, in at his chest and through the middle of his pump and on out at the back, denting a rib. The bullet went on and hit the wall forty-nine inches above the floor, but it was spent and only nicked it. He was on his back, legs stretched out, left arm straight at his side and right arm crossing his chest. Dressed but no jacket, in his shirtsleeves. No disorder, no sign of a struggle. As you said, no gun. Am I going too fast?"

"No."

"Stop me if you have questions. It was the living room of his apartment on the third floor at Sixty-three Arbor Street—two rooms, kitchenette, and bath. He had been living there three years, alone, single, thirty-six years old. He was a free-lance writer, and in the last four years he had done seven articles for *Tick-Tock* magazine. He was going to be married in March to a girl named Marian Hinckley, twenty-four, on the staff of *Tick-Tock*. Of course I could go on. I could have brought the file. But there's nothing in it about his movements or connections or associates that would help. It hasn't helped us."

"You left out a little detail, the caliber of the bullet."

"I didn't leave it out. There was no bullet. It wasn't there."

My eyes widened. "Well. A damned neat murderer."

"Yeah. Neat and coolheaded. Judging from the wound, it was a thirty-eight or bigger. Now two facts. One: for three weeks Althaus had been collecting material for an article on the FBI for *Tick-Tock* magazine, and not a sign of it, nothing, was there in the apartment. Two: about eleven o'clock that Friday night three FBI men left the house at Sixty-three Arbor Street and went around the corner to a car and drove off."

I sat and looked at him. There are various reasons for keeping your mouth shut, but the best one is that you have nothing to say.

"So they killed him," Cramer said. "Did they go there to kill him? Certainly not. There are several ways to figure it. The one I like best is that they rang his number and he wasn't answering the phone, so they thought he was out. They went and rang his bell and he wasn't answering that either, so they opened the door and went in for a bag job. He pulled a gun, and one of them shot before he did. They train them good in that basement in Washington. They looked for what they wanted and got it and left, taking the bullet because it was from one of their guns."

I was listening. I never listened better. I asked, "Did he have a gun?"

"Yes. S and W thirty-eight. He had a permit. It wasn't there. They took it, you'd have to ask them why. There was a box of cartridges, nearly full, in a drawer."

I sat and looked some more, then said, "So you *have* cracked it. Congratulations."

"You'd clown in the hot seat, Goodwin. Do I have to describe it?"

"No. But, after all— Who saw them?"

He shook his head. "I'll give you everything but that. He couldn't help you anyway. He saw them leave the house and go to the car and drive off, and he got the license number. That's how we know and all we know. We're hogtied. Even if we could name them, where would that get us? I've seen plenty of murderers I could name, but so what, if I couldn't prove it. But this one, that goddam outfit, I'd give a year's pay to hook them and make it stick. This isn't their town, it's mine. Ours. The New York Police Department. They've had us gritting our teeth for years. Now, by God, they think they can break and enter people's houses and commit homicide in *my* territory, and laugh at me!"

"Did they? Laugh?"

"Yes. I went to Sixty-ninth Street myself and saw Wragg. I told him that of course they had known that Althaus was collecting material for a piece, and maybe they had had a stake-out on him the night he was killed, and if so I would appreciate some cooperation. He said he would like to help if he could, but they had too many important things to do to bother about a hack muckraker. I didn't tell him they had been seen. He *would* have laughed."

His jaw was working. "Of course it has been discussed in the Commissioner's office. Several times. I'm hogtied. We wouldn't like anything better than hanging it on that bunch of grabbers, but what have we got for a jury, and what could we get? So we lay off. So I say this: I'll not only write a report on Wolfe and you for the Commissioner, I'll see him and talk to him. I don't think you'll lose your licenses. But I won't tell him about seeing you."

He rose and went to the bed and came back with his hat and coat. "You might as well finish the milk. And I hope that Mrs. Bruner gets her money's worth." He put out a hand. "Happy New Year."

"The same to you." I got up and shook. "Could he identify them if it came to that?"

"For God's sake, Goodwin. Three against one?"

"I know. But if it were needed just for a frill, could he?"

"Possibly. He thinks he could. I've given you all I've got. Don't come and don't phone. Give me a few minutes to get out." He started for the door, turned and said, "Give Wolfe my regards," and went.

I finished the milk standing up.

5

It was twenty minutes past noon when I stepped out of the lobby of the Westside Hotel. I felt like walking. For one thing, I was still loose, and it was nice to walk without wondering if I had company. For another thing, I didn't want to think hard on top, and when I walk the hard thinking, if any, is down where it doesn't use words. And for a third thing, I wanted to do some sightseeing. It was a nice sunny winter day, not much wind, and I crossed town to Sixth Avenue and turned south.

To show the kind of thinking that comes on top with no effort when I'm walking, as I crossed Washington Square I was thinking that it was a coincidence that Arbor Street was in the Village and Sarah Dacos lived in the Village. That couldn't be called a hard thought, since a quarter of a million people lived in the Village, more or less, and I have known fancier coincidences, but it's a fair sample of what my mind does when I'm walking.

I had been in Arbor Street before, no matter why for this report. It's narrow and only three blocks long, with an assortment of old brick houses on either side. Number 63, which was near the middle, had nothing distinctive about it. I stood across the street and looked it over. The windows on the third floor, where Morris Althaus had lived and died, had tan drapes that were drawn. I went to the corner around which the G-men had parked their car. As I said, sightseeing, loose. Actually, of course, I was professionally observing the scene of a crime which might be going to have my attention. It helps somehow. Helps me, not Wolfe; he wouldn't go to the window to see the scene of a crime. I would have liked to go up to the third floor for a look at the living room, but I wanted to get home in time for lunch, so I backtracked to Christopher Street and flagged a taxi.

The reason I wanted to be there for lunch was the rule that business must never be mentioned during meals. It was twenty past one when Fritz let me in and I put my coat and hat on the rack, so Wolfe was at the table. Going to the dining room and taking my place across from him, I made a remark about the weather. He grunted and swallowed a bite of braised sweetbread. Fritz came with the dish, and I took some. I was not being merely petty; I was showing him that sometimes rules can be damn silly; one you make so you can enjoy your food can just about spoil a meal. It didn't spoil mine, but there wasn't much conversation.

But there was another reason for saving it. As we

pushed our chairs back I told him I wanted to show him something in the basement, and I led the way to the hall, then to the right, and down the steps. The basement has Fritz's room and bath, a storeroom, and a large room with a pool table. In the last is not only the usual raised bench, but also a big comfortable chair on a platform, for Wolfe when he feels like watching Saul Panzer and me use our cues, which happens about once a year. I led him to that room, flipped the wall switch for light, and spoke.

"Your new office. I hope you like it. There may be only one chance in a million that they can bug a room without getting inside, but that's one too many. Be seated." I lifted my rump onto the rim of the pool table, facing the big chair.

He glared. "Are you badgering me or is it possible?"

"It's conceivable. I wouldn't risk leaking it that Inspector Cramer told me to give you his regards. Also that he bought me a carton of milk, shook my hand, and wished me a happy New Year."

"This is flummery."

"No, sir. It was Cramer."

"In that hotel room?"

"Yes."

He stepped onto the platform and sat. "Report," he growled.

I obeyed. I didn't rush it because I wanted to be sure to get every word in. If we had been in the office he would have leaned back and closed his eyes, but that chair wasn't built for it and he had to stay straight. For the last ten minutes his lips were pressed tight, either because of what he was hearing or of where he was sitting, probably both. I finished with my sightseeing trip and said that a man across the street, maybe walking a dog, or one in a front room of either of two houses, could have seen them leave Number 63 and go around the corner to the car, and even the license number. There was a light at the corner.

He took in a bushel of air through his nose and let it out through his mouth. "I wouldn't have thought," he said, "that Mr. Cramer could be such an ass."

I nodded. "I know it sounds like it. But he didn't know, until I told him, why the FBI was on us. He only knew we had stung them somehow, and he had a murder he couldn't tag them for, and he decided to hand it to you. You've got to admit that you should feel flattered that he thought there was the remotest chance you could pull it, and look at all the trouble he took. And after I told him about Mrs. Bruner he didn't stop to figure it. Probably he has by now. He must realize that it doesn't fit. Suppose you passed a miracle and tied that murder to them so they couldn't shake it off. That wouldn't fill your client's order. The only way that could help her and earn you a fee would be if you said to them, look, I'll lay off on the murder if you'll lay off of Mrs. Bruner. Cramer wouldn't like that, that's not his idea at all. Neither would you, really. Making a deal with a murderer isn't your style. Have I got it straight?"

He grunted. "I don't like your pronouns."

"All right, make it 'we' and 'us.' It's not my style either."

He shook his head. "It's a pickle." A corner of his mouth curled up.

I stared and demanded, "What the hell are you smiling at?"

"The pickle. The alternative. You have made it clear

that it would be futile to establish that the FBI killed that man. Very well, then we'll establish that they didn't."

"Good for us. And then?"

"We'll see." He turned a hand over. "Archie. We had nothing. The items Mr. Cohen gave us were mere trivia, offering not even a forlorn hope. Now, thanks to Mr. Cramer, we have a nut with meat in it, an unsolved murder in which the FBI is deeply involved, whether they committed it or not. An open challenge to ingenuity, to our talents if we have any. We need first to learn, assuredly, who killed that man. You saw Mr. Cramer's face and heard his tone. Is he really satisfied that it was the FBI?"

"Yes."

"Justly?"

"He thinks so. Of course it appeals to him. He refers to them as that goddam outfit and that bunch of grabbers. After he learned about the three G-men being at the scene at the right time he probably let up on other possibilities, but he's a good cop, and if there had been any other lead that was at all hot he would have kept on it, and apparently he didn't. Also, if Althaus was there dead when they entered, why didn't they report it? Anonymously, of course, after they left. They might have preferred not to, but it's a fair question. Also the bullet. Not many murderers would have realized that it had gone on through to the wall and fallen to the floor, and found it and taken it. With an old pro like Cramer that would be a big point. So I guess you could say justly."

He was frowning at me. "Who is the Wragg Mr. Cramer mentioned?"

"Richard Wragg. Top G-man in New York. Special agent in charge."

"Does he know, or believe, that Althaus was killed by one of his men?"

"I'd have to ask him. He could know one of them did, but he couldn't know he didn't, because he wasn't there. He's not a damn fool, and he would be if he believed everything they tell him. Does it matter?"

"It might. It could be of great consequence."

"Then my guess is that he either knows a G-man killed him or he thinks it probable. Otherwise, when Cramer went and asked him for cooperation he would probably have opened up. The FBI likes to oblige local cops when it doesn't cost them anything—prestige, for instance—and Wragg would know that Cramer wouldn't care about their calling at Althaus's place uninvited. Cops do that too, as you know. So Wragg may even have the bullet in a drawer of his desk."

"What is your opinion? Do you agree with Mr. Cramer?"

"That's a strange question, from you. I don't rate an opinion, and you don't either. Maybe the landlord shot Althaus because he was behind on the rent. Or and or and or."

He nodded. "That's what we must explore. You will start now, as you think best. Perhaps with his family. My recollection is that his father, David Althaus, makes clothes for women."

"Right. Seventh Avenue." I slid off of the pool table and was on my feet. "Since we prefer it that he wasn't killed by a G-man, I suppose we're not interested in what he had collected on the FBI."

"We're interested in everything." He made a face.

"And if you find anyone you think I should see, bring him." He made a face again and added, "Or her."

"With pleasure. My first stop will be the *Gazette*, to go through the file, and Lon may have some facts that haven't been printed. As for bringing people, the house may be covered front and back. How do I get them in and out?"

"The door. We are investigating a murder with which the FBI is not concerned. So Mr. Wragg told Mr. Cramer. And for once Mr. Cramer won't complain."

"Then I don't bother about tails?"

"No."

"That's a relief." I went.

6

My watch said 4:35 as I entered a drugstore near
Grand Central, consulted the Manhattan phone book,
went to a booth and shut the door, and dialed a number.

From the *Gazette* files, and from Lon Cohen by word
of mouth off the record, I had filled a dozen pages of
my notebook. I have it here now, but all of it in print
would also take a dozen pages, so I'll report only what
you need to understand what happened. Here are the
principal names:

MORRIS ALTHAUS, deceased, 36, height 5 feet 11,
weight 175, dark complexion, handsome, liked all right
by men but more than liked by women. Had had a
two-year affair, 1962 and 1963, with a certain stage personality, name not given here. Had earned from his
writing around ten grand a year, but it had probably

been augmented by his mother without his father's
knowledge. Not on record when he and Marian Hinckley had decided to tie up, but as far as known he had
had no other girl friend for several months. Three hundred and eighty-four typewritten pages of an unfinished novel had been found in his apartment. No one
at the *Gazette,* including Lon, had any firm guess who
had killed him. No one there had known, before the
murder, that he had been collecting material for a
piece on the FBI, and Lon thought that was a disgrace
to journalism in general and to the *Gazette* personnel
in particular. Apparently Althaus had used rubber
soles.

DAVID ALTHAUS, Morris's father, around 60, was a
partner in Althaus and Greif, makers of the Peggy
Pilgrim line of dresses and suits (see your local newspaper). David had resented it that Morris, his only
child, had given Peggy Pilgrim the go-by, and they
hadn't been close in recent years.

IVANA (Mrs. David) ALTHAUS had not seen a reporter, and would not. She was still, seven weeks after
her son's death, seeing no one but a few close friends.

MARIAN HINCKLEY, 24, had been on the research
staff at *Tick-Tock* for about two years. There were pictures of her in the file, and they made it easy to understand why Althaus had decided to concentrate on her.
She had also refused to talk to reporters, but a newshen
from the *Post* had finally got enough out of her for a
spread, making some fur fly at the *Gazette.* It had
made one *Gazette* female so sore that she worked up
the theory that Marian Hinckley had shot Althaus with
his own gun because he was cheating on her, but it
had petered out.

Timothy Quayle, around 40, was a senior editor at *Tick-Tock*. I include him because he had got rough and tangled with a journalist from the *Daily News* who tried to corner Marian Hinckley in the lobby of the *Tick-Tock* building. A man that gallant deserves a look.

Vincent Yarmack, around 50, was another senior editor at *Tick-Tock*. I include him because the piece by Althaus about the FBI had been his project.

It didn't look very promising for an approach. I considered the stage personality, but her whirl with Althaus had ended more than a year ago, and besides, a couple of previous experiences had taught me that actresses are better from the fifth or sixth row. The two editors would hang up. Father probably had nothing. Marian Hinckley would stiff-neck me. The best bet was mother, and it was her number I looked up and went to the booth to dial.

First, of course, to get her to the phone. To the female who answered I gave no name; I merely told her, in an official tone, to tell Mrs. Althaus that I was talking from a booth and an FBI man was with me and I must speak to her. It worked. In a couple of minutes another voice came.

"Who is this? An FBI man?"

"Mrs. Althaus?"

"Yes."

"My name is Archie Goodwin. I'm not an FBI man. I work for Nero Wolfe, the private investigator. The FBI man is not here in the booth with me; he is with me because he is following me. Tailing me. He will follow me to your address, but that doesn't matter to me if it doesn't to you. I must see you—now, if possible. It will—"

"I am not seeing anybody."

"I know. You may have heard of Nero Wolfe. Have you?"

"Yes."

"He has been told by a man he knows well that your son Morris was killed by an agent of the FBI. That's why I am being followed. And that's why I must see you. I can be there in ten minutes. Did you get my name? Archie Goodwin."

Silence. Finally: "You *know* who killed my son?"

"Not his name. I don't *know* anything. I only know what Mr. Wolfe has been told. That's all I can say on the phone. If I may make a suggestion, we think Miss Marian Hinckley should know about this too. Perhaps you could phone her and ask her to come, and I can tell both of you. Could you?"

"I could, yes. Are you a newspaper reporter? Is this a trick?"

"No. If I were this would be pretty dumb, you'd only have me bounced. I'm Archie Goodwin."

"But I don't . . ." Long pause. "Very well. The hall-man will ask you for identification."

I told her of course, and hung up before she could change her mind.

When leaving the house I had decided that I would completely ignore the tail question, but I couldn't help it if my eyes, while scouting the street for an empty taxi, took notice of standing vehicles. However, when I was in and rolling, up Madison Avenue and then Park, I kept facing front. To hell with the rear.

It was a regulation Park Avenue hive in the Eighties—marquee, doorman hopping out when the taxi stopped, rubber runner saving the rug in the lobby—

but it was Grade A, because the doorman did not double as hallman. When I showed the hallman, who was expecting me, my private investigator license he gave it a good look, handed it back, and told me 10B, and I went to the elevator. On the tenth floor I was admitted by a uniformed female who took my hat and coat, put them in a closet, and conducted me through an arch into a room even bigger than Lily Rowan's, where twenty couples can dance. I have a test for people with rooms that big—not the rugs or the furniture or the drapes, but the pictures on the walls. If I can tell what they are, okay. If all I can do is guess, look out; these people will bear watching. That room passed the test fine. I was looking at a canvas showing three girls sitting on the grass under a tree when footsteps came and I turned. She approached. She didn't offer a hand, but she said in a low, soft voice, "Mr. Goodwin? I'm Ivana Althaus," and moved to a chair.

Even without the picture test I would have passed her—her small slender figure with its honest angles, her hair with its honest gray, her eyes with their honest doubt. As I turned a chair to sit facing her I decided to be as honest as possible. She was saying that Miss Hinckley would come soon, but she would prefer not to wait. She had understood me to say on the phone that her son had been killed by an agent of the FBI. Was that correct?

Her eyes were straight at me, and I met them. "Not strictly," I told her. "I said that someone told Mr. Wolfe that. I should explain about Mr. Wolfe. He is— uh—eccentric, and he has certain strong feelings about the New York Police Department. He resents their attitude toward him and his work, and he thinks they interfere too much. He reads the newspapers, and especially news about murders, and a couple of weeks ago he got the idea that the police and the District Attorney were letting go on the murder of your son, and when he learned that your son had been collecting material for an article about the FBI he suspected that the letting go might be deliberate. If so, it might be a chance to give the police a black eye, and nothing would please him better."

Her eyes were staying straight at me, hardly a blink. "So," I said, "we had no case on our hands, and he started some inquiries. One thing we learned, a fact that hasn't been published, was that nothing about the FBI, no notes or documents, was found by the police in your son's apartment. Perhaps you knew that."

She nodded. "Yes."

"I supposed you did, so I mentioned it. We have learned some other facts which I have been instructed not to mention. You'll understand that. Mr. Wolfe wants to save them until he has enough to act on. But yesterday afternoon a man told him that he knows that an FBI agent killed your son, and he backed it up with some information. I won't give you his name, or the information, but he's a reliable man and the information is solid, though it isn't enough to prove it. So Mr. Wolfe wants all he can get from people who were close to your son—for instance, people to whom he may have told things he had learned about the FBI. Of course you are one of them, and so is Miss Hinckley. And Mr. Yarmack. I was told to make it clear to you that Mr. Wolfe is not looking for a client or a fee. He is doing this on his own and doesn't want or expect anyone to pay him."

Her eyes were still on me, but her mind wasn't. She was considering something. "I see no reason . . ." she said, and stopped.

I waited a little, then said, "Yes, Mrs. Althaus?"

"I see no reason why I shouldn't tell you. I have suspected it was the FBI, ever since Mr. Yarmack told me that nothing about them was found in the apartment. So has Mr. Yarmack, and so has Miss Hinckley. I don't think I am a vindictive woman, Mr. Goodwin, but he was my—" Her voice was going to quiver, and she stopped. In a moment she went on. "He was my son. I am still trying to realize that he—he's gone. Did you know him? Did you ever meet him?"

"No."

"You're a detective."

"Yes."

"You're expecting me to help you find—to fix the blame for my son's death. Very well, I want to. But I don't think I can. He rarely spoke to me about his work. I don't remember that he ever mentioned the FBI. Miss Hinckley has asked me that, and Mr. Yarmack. I'm sorry I can't tell you anything about it, I'm truly sorry, because if they killed him I hope they will be punished. It says in Leviticus 'Thou shalt not avenge,' but Aristotle wrote that revenge is just. You see, I have been thinking about it. I believe—"

She turned to face the arch. A door had closed, and there were voices, and then a girl appeared. As she approached I got up, but Mrs. Althaus kept her chair. The pictures in the *Gazette* file understated it. Marian Hinckley was a dish. She was an in-between, neither blonde nor brunette, brown hair and blue eyes, and she moved straight and smooth. If she wore a hat she had ditched it in the foyer. She came and gave Mrs. Althaus a cheek kiss, then turned to look at me as Mrs. Althaus pronounced my name. As the blue eyes took me in I instructed mine to ignore any aspect of the situation that was irrelevant to the job. When Mrs. Althaus invited her to sit I moved a chair up. As she sat she spoke to Mrs. Althaus. "If I understood you on the phone—did you say Nero Wolfe knows it was the FBI? Was that it?"

"I'm afraid I didn't get it straight," Mrs. Althaus said. "Will you tell her, Mr. Goodwin?"

I described it, the three points: why Wolfe was interested, what had made him suspicious, and how his suspicion had been supported by what a man told him yesterday. I explained that he didn't *know* it was the FBI, and he certainly couldn't prove it, but he intended to try to and that was why I was there.

Miss Hinckley was frowning at me. "But I don't see . . . Has he told the police what the man told him?"

"I'm sorry," I said, "I guess I didn't make it plain enough. He thinks the police know it was the FBI, or suspect it. For instance, one thing he wants to ask you people: Are the police keeping after you? Coming back, again and again, asking the same questions over and over? Mrs. Althaus?"

"No."

"Miss Hinckley?"

"No. But we've told them everything we know."

"That doesn't matter. In a murder investigation, if they haven't got a line they like, they never let up on anybody, and it looks as if they have let up on everybody. That's one thing we need to know. Mrs. Althaus

just told me that you and Mr. Yarmack both think that
the FBI killed him. Is that correct?"

"Yes. Yes, it is. Because there was nothing about the
FBI in his apartment."

"Do you know what there might have been? What
he had dug up?"

"No. Morris never told me about things like that."

"Does Mr. Yarmack know?"

"I don't know. I don't think so."

"How do you feel about it, Miss Hinckley? Whoever
killed Morris Althaus, do you want him caught? Caught
and dealt with?"

"Of course I do. Certainly I do."

I turned to Mrs. Althaus. "You do too. All right, it's a
good bet that he never *will* be caught unless Nero
Wolfe does it. You may know that he doesn't go to see
people. You'll have to go to him, to his house—you and
Miss Hinckley, and, if possible, Mr. Yarmack. Can you
be there this evening at nine o'clock?"

"Why . . ." She had her hands clasped. "I don't . . .
What good would it do? There's nothing I can tell him."

"There might be. I often think there's nothing *I* can
tell him, but I find out I'm wrong. Or if he only decides
that none of you can tell him anything, that will help.
Will you come?"

"I suppose . . ." She looked at the girl who had been
expecting to be her daughter-in-law.

"Yes," Miss Hinckley said. "I'll go."

I could have hugged her. It would have been relevant to the job. I asked her, "Could you bring Mr.
Yarmack?"

"I don't know. I'll try."

"Good." I rose. "The address is in the phone book."

To Mrs. Althaus: "I should tell you, it's next to certain that the FBI has a watch on the house and you will be seen. If you don't mind, Mr. Wolfe doesn't. He's perfectly willing for them to know he is investigating the murder of your son. Nine o'clock?"

She said yes, and I went. In the foyer the maid came and wanted to hold my coat, and not to hurt her feelings I let her. Down in the lobby, from the look the doorman gave me as he opened the door I deduced that the hallman had told him what I was, and to be in character I met the look with a sharp and wary eye. Outside, some snowflakes were doing stunts. In the taxi, headed downtown, again I ignored the rear. I figured that if they were on me, which was highly likely, maybe one cent of each ten grand of Wolfe's income tax, and one mill of each ten grand of mine, would go to pay government employees to keep me company uninvited, which didn't seem right.

Wolfe had just come down from the plant rooms after his four-to-six afternoon session with the orchids and got nicely settled in his chair with *The Treasure of Our Tongue*. Instead of going on in and crossing to my desk as usual, I stopped at the sill of the office door, and when he looked up I pointed a finger straight down, emphatically, turned, and beat it to the stairs to the basement and on down. Flipping the light switch, I went and perched on the pool table. Two minutes. Three. Four, and there were footsteps. He stood at the door, glared at me, and spoke.

"I won't tolerate this."

I raised an eyebrow. "I could write it."

"Pfui. Two points. One, the risk is extremely slight. Two, we can use it. As you talk you can insert com-

ments or statements at will which I am to disregard,
notifying me by raising a finger. I shall do the same.
Of course making no reference to Mr. Cramer; we
can't risk that; and maintaining our conclusion that the
FBI killed that man, and we intend to establish it."

"But actually we don't."

"Certainly not." He turned and went.

So I was foxed. His house, his office, and his chair.
But I had to admit, as I mounted the steps, that pig-
headed as he was, it wasn't a bad idea. If they really
had an electronic ear on the office, which I didn't believe, it might even be a damned good idea. When I
entered the office he was back at his desk and I went
to mine, and as I sat he said, "Well?"

He should have had a finger raised. He never wastes
breath by saying "Well?" when I return from an errand; he merely puts the book down, or the beer glass,
and is ready for me to speak.

I raised a finger. "Your guess that they might have
hit on the FBI theory at the *Gazette,* and be working
on it, wasn't so good." I lowered the finger. "Lon Cohen
didn't mention it, so I didn't. They haven't got a theory.
He let me go through the files, and we talked, and I
got a dozen pages of names and assorted details, some
of which might possibly be useful." I raised a finger.
"I'll type it up at the usual five dollars a page." I lowered the finger. "Next I phoned Mrs. David Althaus
from a booth, and she said she would see me, and I
went. Park Avenue in the Eighties, tenth-floor apartment, all the trimmings you would expect. Pictures
okay. I won't describe her because you'll see her. She
quotes Leviticus and Aristotle." Finger raised. "I
wanted to quote Plato but couldn't work it in." Finger

lowered. "I had asked her on the phone to ask Marian Hinckley to come, and she said she would be there soon. She said she had understood me to say on the phone that her son had been killed by an agent of the FBI and was that correct. From there on you had better have it verbatim."

I gave it to him, straight through, knowing that I had said nothing we wouldn't be willing for the FBI to hear. Leaning back with his eyes closed, he wouldn't have been able to see a raised finger, so I couldn't make any insertions. When I finished he grunted, opened his eyes, and said, "It's bad enough when you know there's a needle in the haystack. When you don't even—"

The doorbell rang. Going to the hall for a look, I saw a G-man on the stoop. Not that I recognized him, but it must be—the right age, the broad shoulders, the manly mug with a firm jaw, the neat dark gray coat. I went and opened the door the two inches allowed by the chain bolt and said, "Yes, sir?"

He blurted through the crack, "My name's Quayle and I want to see Nero Wolfe!"

"Spell it, please?"

"Timothy Quayle! Q,U,A,Y,L,E!"

"Mr. Wolfe is engaged. I'll see."

I went to the office door. "One of the names in my notebook. Timothy Quayle. Senior editor at *Tick-Tock* magazine. The hero type. He slugged a reporter who was annoying Marian Hinckley. She must have phoned him about you soon after I left."

"No," he growled.

"It's half an hour till dinner. Are you in the middle of a chapter?"

He glowered at me. "Bring him."

I returned to the front, slid the bolt, and swung the door open, and he entered. As I was shutting the door he told me I was Archie Goodwin, and I conceded it, took care of his coat and hat, and led him to the office. Three steps in he stopped to glance around, aimed the glance at Wolfe, and demanded, "Did you get my name?"

Wolfe nodded. "Mr. Quayle."

He advanced to the desk. "I am a friend of Miss Marian Hinckley. I want to know what kind of a game you're playing. I want an explanation."

"Bah," Wolfe said.

"Don't bah me! What are you up to?"

"This is ridiculous," Wolfe said. "I like eyes at a level. If you can only blather at me, Mr. Goodwin will put you out. If you will take that chair, change your tone, and give me an acceptable reason why I should account to you, I may listen."

Quayle opened his mouth and shut it again. He turned his head to look at me, there on my feet, apparently to see if I was man enough. I would have liked it just as well if he had decided I wasn't, for after that night and day I would have welcomed an excuse to twist another arm. But he vetoed it, went to the red leather chair and sat, and scowled at Wolfe. "I know about you," he said. Not so blathery, but not at all sociable. "I know how you operate. If you want to hook Mrs. Althaus for some change, that's her lookout, but you're not going to drag Miss Hinckley in. I don't intend—"

"Archie," Wolfe snapped. "Put him out. Fritz will open the door." He pushed a button.

I stepped to about arm's length from the red leather chair and stood looking down at the hero. Fritz came, and Wolfe told him to hold the front door open, and he went.

Quayle's situation was bad. With me standing there in front of him, if he started to leave the chair I could get about any hold I wanted while he was coming up. But my situation was bad too. Removing a 180-pound man from a padded armchair is a problem, and he had savvy enough to stay put, leaning back. But his feet weren't pulled in enough. I started my hands for his shoulders, then dived and got his ankles and yanked and kept going, and had him in the hall, on his back, before he could even try to counter, and then the damn fool tried to turn to get hand leverage on the floor. At the front door I braked when Fritz got his arms and held them down.

"There's snow on the stoop," I said. "If I let you up and give you your hat and coat, just walk out. I know more tricks than you do. Right?"

"Yes. You goddam goon."

"Goodwin. You left out the D, W, I, but I'll overlook it. All right, Fritz."

We let go, and he scrambled to his feet. Fritz got his coat from the rack, but he said, "I want to go back in. I'm going to ask him something."

"No. You have bad manners. We'd have to bounce you again."

"No you wouldn't. I want to *ask* him something."

"Politely. Tactfully."

"Yes."

I shut the door. "You can have two minutes. Don't

sit down, don't raise your voice, and don't use words like 'goon.' Lead the way, Fritz."

We filed down the hall and in, Fritz in front and me in the rear. Wolfe, whose good ears hear what is said in the hall, gave him a cold eye as he stopped short of the desk, surrounded by Fritz and me.

"You wanted an acceptable reason," he told Wolfe. "As I said, I am a friend of Miss Hinckley. A good enough friend so that she called me on the phone to tell me about Goodwin—what he said to her and Mrs. Althaus. I advised her not to come here this evening, but she's coming. At nine o'clock?"

"Yes."

"Then I'm going—" He stopped. That wasn't the way. It came hard, but he managed it. "I want to be here. Will you . . . May I come?"

"If you control yourself."

"I will."

"Time's up," I said, and took his arm to turn him.

7

At ten minutes past nine in the evening of that long day I went to the kitchen. Wolfe was at the center table with Fritz, arguing about the number of juniper berries to put in a marinade for venison loin chops. Knowing that that could go on and on, I said, "Excuse me. They're all here, and more. David Althaus, the father, came along. He's the bald one, to your right at the back. Also a lawyer named Bernard Fromm, to your left at the back. Long-headed and hard-eyed."

Wolfe frowned. "I don't want him."

"Of course not. Shall I tell him so?"

"Confound it." He turned to Fritz. "Very well, proceed. I say three, but proceed as you will. If you put in five I won't even have to taste it; the smell will tell me. With four it might be palatable." He gave me a nod and I headed for the office, and he followed.

He circled around Mrs. Althaus in the red leather chair and stood while I pronounced names. There were two rows of yellow chairs, with Vincent Yarmack, Marian Hinckley, and Timothy Quayle in front, and David Althaus and Bernard Fromm in the rear. That put Quayle nearest me, which had seemed advisable. Wolfe sat, sent his eyes left to right and back again, and spoke. "I should tell you that it may be that with an electronic eavesdropping device agents of the Federal Bureau of Investigation hear everything that is said in this room. Mr. Goodwin and I think it unlikely, but it is quite possible. I feel that you—"

"Why would they?" Fromm the lawyer. The courtroom tone, cross-examination.

"That will appear, Mr. Fromm. I feel that you should be aware of that possibility, however remote. Now I beg you to indulge me. I'm going to talk a while. I can expect you to help further my interest only if I can demonstrate that your interest runs with mine. You are the father, the mother, the fiancée, and the associates of a man who was murdered seven weeks ago, and the murderer has not been exposed. I intend to expose him. I intend to establish that Morris Althaus was killed by an agent of the Federal Bureau of Investigation. That intention—"

They made two demands simultaneously. Yarmack demanded, "How?" and Fromm demanded, "Why?"

Wolfe nodded. "That intention stands on two legs. Recently I undertook a job which made it necessary for me to make inquiries regarding certain activities of the FBI, and they retaliated immediately by trying to have me deprived of my license as a private investigator. They may succeed; but even if they do, as a private citizen I can pursue an investigation in my private interest, and it will certainly be in my interest to discredit their pretension that they are faultless champions of law and justice. That's one leg. The other leg is my long-standing grievance against the Homicide Squad of the New York Police Department. They too have pretensions. On numerous occasions they have hampered my legitimate activities. They have threatened more than once to prosecute me for withholding evidence or obstructing justice. It would be gratifying to me to reciprocate, to demonstrate that they know or suspect that the FBI is implicated in a murder and *they* are obstructing justice. That would also—"

"You're talking plenty," Fromm cut in. "Can you back it up?"

"By inference, yes. The police and the District Attorney know that Morris Althaus had been collecting material for an article about the FBI, but they found no such material in his apartment. Mr. Yarmack. I believe you were involved in that project?"

Vincent Yarmack was more my idea of a senior editor than Timothy Quayle—round sloping shoulders, tight little mouth, and eyes so pale you had to guess they were there behind the black-rimmed cheaters.

"I was," he said in a voice that was close to a squeak.

"And Mr. Althaus *had* collected material?"

"Certainly."

"Had he turned it over to you, or was it in his possession?"

"I thought it was in his possession. But I have been told by the police that there was nothing about the FBI in his apartment."

"Didn't you draw an inference from that?"

"Well . . . one inference was obvious, that someone had taken it. It wasn't likely that Morris had put it somewhere else."

"Mrs. Althaus told Mr. Goodwin this afternoon that you suspected it was the FBI. Is that correct?"

Yarmack turned his head for a glance at Mrs. Althaus, and back to Wolfe. "I may have given her that impression in a private conversation. This conversation isn't very private, according to you."

Wolfe grunted. "I said the eavesdropping is possible but not verified. If you drew that inference, certainly the police would." His eyes moved. "Wouldn't they, Mr. Fromm?"

The lawyer nodded. "Presumably. But that doesn't warrant a conclusion that they are obstructing justice."

"A conclusion, no. A surmise, yes. If not obstruction, at least nonfeasance. As a member of the bar, you are aware of the tenacity of the police and the District Attorney in an unsolved murder case. If they—"

"I don't practice criminal law."

"Pfui. Surely you are aware of what every child knows. If they were not satisfied with the assumption that the FBI is responsible for the disappearance of that material and therefore was probably involved in the murder, they would certainly be exploring other possibilities—for instance, Mr. Yarmack. Are they, Mr. Yarmack? Are they harassing you?"

The editor stared. "Harassing me? What about?"

"The possibility that you killed Morris Althaus and took that material. Don't erupt. Many murders have prompted less plausible theories. He told you of a discovery he had made and evidence he had obtained which, perhaps unknown to him, was in some way a mortal threat to you, and you removed him and the evidence. An excellent theory. Surely—"

"Tommyrot. Absolute tommyrot."

"To you, perhaps. But surely, in a muddle with an unsolved murder, they would dog you; but they don't. I am not accusing you of murder, sir, not at the moment; I am merely showing that the police are either shirking or slighting their duty. Unless you have given them an impregnable alibi for the night of November twentieth. Have you?"

"No. Impregnable, no."

"Have you, Mr. Quayle?"

"Nuts," Quayle said. Bad manners again.

Wolfe eyed him. "You are here by sufferance. You wanted to know what I am up to. I am making that clear. Impelled solely by my private interest, I hope to disclose the implication of the FBI in a murder and the failure of the police to do their duty. In that effort I must guard against the danger of being balked by circumstance. Yesterday I received in confidence information strongly indicating the guilt of the FBI, but it is not conclusive. I dare not ignore the possibility that the apparent inaction of the police is merely tactical, that they and the FBI both know the identity of the murderer, and that they are holding off until they have decisive evidence. I must be fully satisfied on that point before I move. You can help to satisfy me, and if instead you choose to flout me I don't want you here. Mr. Goodwin has ejected you once and he can do so again if necessary. He would be even more effective with an audience; he likes an audience as well as I do. If you prefer to stay, I asked you a question."

Quayle's jaw was set. The poor guy was in a fix.

Seated next to him, so close he could have reached out and touched her, was the girl for whom and before whom he had pitched into a nosy newshound, begging Lon Cohen's pardon, and now he was being crowded by a nosy bloodhound. I expected him to turn his head, either to her to show that for her sake he could swallow even his pride, or to me to show that I was really no problem, but he stayed focused on Wolfe.

"I told you I would control myself," he said. "All right. I have no impregnable alibi for the night of November twentieth. That answers your question, and now I ask one. How do you expect Miss Hinckley to help to satisfy you?"

Wolfe nodded. "That's reasonable and relevant. Miss Hinckley, manifestly you are willing to help or you wouldn't be here. I have suggested a theory to account for the guilt of Mr. Yarmack; now one for Mr. Quayle. That's simple. Millions of men have killed a fellow man because of a woman—to spite her or bereave her or get her. If Mr. Quayle killed your fiancé do you want him exposed?"

She lifted her hands and let them drop. "But that's ridiculous."

"Not at all. To the family and friends of most murderers the imputation seems ridiculous, but that doesn't make it so. I am not imputing guilt to Mr. Quayle; I am merely considering possibilities. Have you any reason to suppose that your betrothal to Mr. Althaus displeased him?"

"You can't expect me to answer that."

"I'll answer it," Quayle blurted. "Yes. It displeased me."

"Indeed. By right? Was it a trespass?"

"I don't know about 'right.' I had asked Miss Hinckley to marry me. I had ex— I had hoped she would."

"Had she agreed to?"

The lawyer cut in. "Take it easy, Wolfe. You mentioned trespass. I think you're trespassing. I'm here at the request of Mr. Althaus, my client, and I'm not entitled to speak on behalf of Miss Hinckley or Mr. Quayle, but I think you're overreaching. I know your reputation. I know you're not a jobber, and I won't challenge your bona fides unless I have reason, but as an attorney-at-law I have to say you're spreading it pretty thick. Or perhaps I mean thin. Mr. Althaus, and his wife, and I as his attorney, certainly want to see justice done. But if you have received information strongly indicating the guilt of the FBI, why this inquisition?"

"I thought I made that plain."

"As an explanation of a position, yes, or as a brief for prudence. Not as an excuse for an inquisition of persons. Next you will be asking me if Morris had caught me committing a felony."

"Had he?"

"I'm not going to fill a role in a burlesque. I repeat, you're overreaching."

"Then I'll pull in, but I shall not abandon prudence. I'll ask you this, a routine question in any case of death by violence: If the FBI didn't kill Morris Althaus, who did? Assume that the FBI is definitely cleared and I am the District Attorney. Who had reason to want that man dead? Who hated him or feared him or had something to gain? Can you suggest a name?"

"No. I have considered that, naturally. No."

Wolfe's eyes went right and left. "Can any of you?"

Two of them shook their heads. No one said anything.

"The question is routine," Wolfe said, "but it is not always futile. I ask you to reflect. Without regard for slander; you will not be quoted. Surely Morris Althaus did not live thirty-six years without giving offense to anyone. He offended his father. He offended Mr. Quayle." He looked at Yarmack. "Were the articles he wrote for your magazine innocuous?"

"No," the editor said. "But if they hurt anyone enough for them to murder him I shouldn't think they would wait until now."

"One of them had to wait," Quayle said. "He was in jail."

Wolfe switched editors. "For what?"

"Fraud. A shady real-estate deal. Morris did a piece we called 'The Realty Racket,' and it started an investigation, and one of them got nailed. He was sent up for two years. That was two years ago, a little less, but with time off for good behavior he must be out by now. But he's no murderer, he wouldn't have the guts. I saw him a couple of times when he was trying to get us to leave his name out. He's just a small-time smoothie."

"His name?"

"I don't— Yes, I do. Does it matter? Odell. Something Odell. Frank, that's it. Frank Odell."

"I don't understand—" Mrs. Althaus began, but it came out hoarse and she cleared her throat. She was looking at Wolfe. "I don't understand all this. If it was the FBI, why are you asking all these questions? Why don't you ask Mr. Yarmack what Morris had found out

about the FBI? I have asked him, and he says he
doesn't know."

"I don't," Yarmack said.

Wolfe nodded. "So I assumed. Otherwise you would
be harassed not only by the police. Had he told you
nothing of his discoveries and conjectures?"

"No. He never did. He waited until he had a first
draft. That was how he always worked."

Wolfe grunted. "Madam," he told Mrs. Althaus, "as
I said, I must be satisfied. I should ask a thousand
questions—all night, all week. The Federal Bureau of
Investigation is a formidable foe, entrenched in power
and privilege. It is not rodomontade but merely a
statement of fact to say that no individual or group in
America would undertake the job I have assigned myself. If an agent of the FBI killed your son there is
not the slightest chance that he will be brought to account unless I do it. Therefore the choice of procedure
is exclusively mine. Is that overreaching, Mr. Fromm?"

"No," the lawyer said. "It would be unrealistic not
to agree with you about the FBI. When I learned that
nothing about them was found in the apartment I
made the obvious assumption, and I told Mr. Althaus
that I thought it very unlikely that the murderer would
ever be caught. The FBI is untouchable. Goodwin told
Mrs. Althaus that a man told you yesterday that he
knows that an FBI agent killed her son, and that he
supported it with information, and I came here intending to demand the man's name and the information,
but you're right. The procedure is up to you. I think it's
hopeless, but I wish you luck, and I wish I could help."

"So do I." Wolfe pushed his chair back and rose.
"It's possible, if this conversation has been overheard,

that one or more of you *will* be harassed. If so I would
like to know. I would like to know of any develop-
ment that comes to your knowledge, however trivial.
Whether the conversation was overheard or not, this
house is under surveillance, and the FBI now knows
that I am concerning myself with the murder of Morris Althaus. The police do not, as far as I know, and I
request you not to tell them; that would only make it
more difficult. I apologize for not offering you refreshment; I was preoccupied. Mr. Althaus, you have not
spoken. Do you wish to?"

"No," David Althaus said—his one and only word.

"Then good evening." Wolfe walked out.

As they left their chairs and moved toward the hall
I stood. The gentlemen could help the ladies with their
coats; I wasn't needed. I must have been about as low
as you can get, for it didn't occur to me that it would
be a pleasure to hold Miss Hinckley's coat until I heard
the front door open, and then it was too late. I stayed
put until I heard it close and then went and bolted it.
They were down on the sidewalk.

I hadn't heard the elevator, so Wolfe must be in the
kitchen, and I headed for it. But he wasn't. Neither
was Fritz. Had he actually climbed the stairs? Why?
The only other way was down. I chose that, and as I
descended I heard his voice. It came from the open
door to Fritz's room, and I stepped to it and entered.

Fritz could have had a room upstairs, but he prefers
the basement. His den is as big as the office and front
room combined, but over the years it has got pretty
cluttered—tables with stacks of magazines, busts of
Escoffier and Brillat-Savarin on stands, framed menus
on the walls, a king-size bed, five chairs, shelves of

books (he has 289 cookbooks), a head of a wild boar he shot in the Vosges, a TV and stereo cabinet, two large cases of ancient cooking vessels, one of which he thinks was used by Julius Caesar's chef, and so on.

Wolfe was in the biggest chair by a table, with a bottle of beer and a glass. Fritz, seated across from him, got up as I entered, but I moved another chair up.

"It's too bad," I said, "that the elevator doesn't come down. Maybe we can have it done."

Wolfe drank beer, put the glass down, and licked his lips. "I want to know," he said, "about those electronic abominations. Could we be heard here?"

"I don't know. I've read about a thing that is supposed to pick up voices half a mile off, but I don't know about how much area it covers or about obstructions like walls and floors. There could be items I haven't read about that can take a whole house. If there aren't there soon will be. People will have to talk with their hands."

He glared at me. Since I had done nothing to deserve it, I glared back. "You realize," he said, "that absolute privacy has never been so imperative."

"I do. God knows I do."

"Could whispers be heard?"

"No. A billion to one. To nothing."

"Then we'll whisper."

"That would cramp your style. If Fritz turns the television on, fairly loud, and we sit close and don't yell, that will do it."

"We could do that in the office."

"Yes, sir."

"Why the devil didn't you suggest it?"

I nodded. "You're in a stew. So am I. I'm surprised

I thought of it now. Let's try it here. In the office I'd have to lean across your desk."

He turned. "If you please, Fritz. It doesn't matter what."

Fritz went to the cabinet and turned a knob, and soon a woman was telling a man she was sorry she had ever met him. He asked (not the man, Fritz) if it was loud enough, and I said a little louder and moved my chair nearer Wolfe. He leaned forward and growled, eighteen inches from my ear, "We'll prepare for a contingency. Do you know if the Ten for Aristology is still in existence?"

My shoulders went up and down. It takes a moron or a genius to ask a question that has no bearing whatever. "No," I said. "That was seven years ago. It probably is. I can ring Lewis Hewitt."

"Not from here."

"I'll go to a booth. Now?"

"Yes. If he says that group still— No. Whatever he says about the Ten for Aristology, ask him if I may call on him tomorrow morning to consult him on an urgent private matter. If he invites me to lunch, as he will, accept."

"He lives on Long Island the year around."

"I know he does."

"We'll probably have to lose a tail."

"We won't need to. If I am seen going to him so much the better."

"Then why not call him from here?"

"Because I'm willing, I even wish, to have my visit to him known, but not that I invited myself."

"What if he can't make it tomorrow?"

"Then as soon as possible."

I went. As I mounted to the hall and got my coat and hat and let myself out and headed for Ninth Avenue, I was thinking, two rules down the drain in one day—the morning schedule and not leaving the house on business—and why? The Ten for Aristology was a bunch of ten well-heeled men who were, to quote, "pursuing the ideal of perfection in food and drink." Seven years back, at the home of one of them, Benjamin Schriver, the shipping tycoon, they had met to pursue their ideal by eating and drinking, and Lewis Hewitt, a member, had arranged with Wolfe for Fritz to cook the dinner. Naturally Wolfe and I had been invited and had gone, and the guy between us at the table had been fed arsenic with the first course, caviar on blinis topped with sour cream, and had died. Quite a party. It had not affected Wolfe's relations with Lewis Hewitt, who was still grateful for a special favor Wolfe had done him long ago, who had a hundred-foot-long orchid house at his Long Island estate, and who came to dinner at the old brownstone about twice a year.

It took a while to get him because the call had to be switched to the greenhouse or the stables or maybe the john, but it was a pleasure for him to hear my voice; he said so. When I told him Wolfe would like to pay him a call he said he would be delighted and that of course we would lunch with him, and added that he would like to ask Wolfe a question regarding the lunch.

"I'm afraid I'll have to do," I told him. "I'm calling from a booth in a drugstore. Excuse my glove, but is there any chance that someone is on an extension?"

"Why—why no. There would be no reason . . ."

"Okay. I'm calling from a booth because our wire is

tapped and Mr. Wolfe doesn't want it known that he suggested calling on you. So don't ring our number. It's conceivable that you might get a call tomorrow afternoon from someone who says he's a reporter and wants to ask questions. I mention it now because I might forget to tomorrow. The idea is, this appointment, our coming to lunch tomorrow, was made last week. All right?"

"Yes, of course. But good heavens, if you know your phone is tapped—isn't that illegal?"

"Sure, that's why it's fun. We'll tell you about it tomorrow—I *guess* we will."

He said he would save his curiosity for tomorrow and would expect us by noon.

There is a TV set and a radio in the office, and when I got back I was expecting to see Wolfe there in his favorite chair, probably with the radio going, but the office was empty, so I proceeded to the rear and down to the basement and found him where I had left him. The television was still on, and Fritz was sitting watching it, yawning. Wolfe was leaning back with his eyes shut, and his lips were going, pushing out and then in, out and in. So he was working, but on what? I stood and looked at him. That's the one thing I never break in on, the lip operation, but that time I had to clamp my jaw to keep my mouth shut because I didn't believe it. There was absolutely nothing he could be hatching. Two full minutes. Three. I decided he was only practicing, it was a dry run, went to a chair, sat, and coughed loud. In a moment he opened his eyes, blinked at me, and straightened up.

I moved my chair closer. "All set," I said. "We're expected by noon, so we should roll by ten-thirty."

"You're not going," he growled. "I telephoned Saul. He'll come at nine."

"Oh. I see. You want me here in case Wragg sends them to confess."

"I want you to find Frank Odell."

"For God's sake. Is *that* what your lips squeezed out."

"No." He turned his head. "A little louder, Fritz." Back to me: "I said after lunch that you had made it clear that it would be futile to establish that the FBI committed that murder. I retract that. I will not bow to futility. We must arrange a situation in which none of the three alternatives would be futile. They are: one, establish that the FBI committed the murder; two, establish that they didn't; and three, establish neither one, let the murder go. We prefer by far the second alternative, and that is why you are to find Frank Odell, but if we are forced to accept the first or the third we must manage circumstances so that we will nevertheless be in a position to fulfill our obligation to our client."

"You have no obligation except to investigate and use your best efforts."

"Your pronouns again."

"All right, 'we' and 'our.'"

"That's better. Just so, our best efforts. The strongest obligation possible for a man with self-esteem, and we both have our full share of that. One point is vital. No matter which alternative circumstances compel us to accept, Mr. Wragg must believe, or at least suspect, that one of his men killed Morris Althaus. I can contrive no maneuver by us that would contribute to that; I was trying to when you returned. Can you?"

"No. He either believes it or he doesn't. Ten to one he does."

"At least we have the odds. Now. I need suggestions regarding the arrangement I intend to make with Mr. Hewitt tomorrow. It will take time, and I'm dry. Fritz?"

No response. I turned. He was sound asleep in the chair, probably snoring, but if so the TV covered it. I suggested moving to the office and trying some WQXR music for a change, and Wolfe agreed, so we woke Fritz and thanked him for his hospitality and told him good night. On the way to the office I stopped off for beer for Wolfe and milk for me, and when I joined him he had the radio going and was back of his desk. Since it was going to take time I brought a yellow chair and put it near his. He poured beer, and I took a swallow of milk and said, "I forgot to say that I didn't ask Hewitt about the Ten for Aristology. You wanted to see him anyway and you can ask him tomorrow. And the program?"

He spoke.

It was well after midnight when he went to the elevator and I went to get the sheets and blankets and pillow for my second night on the couch.

8

There were more than a hundred Odells in the phone books of the five boroughs, but no Frank. That established, I sat at my desk at half past nine Friday morning and considered recourses. It wasn't the kind of problem to discuss with Wolfe, and anyway he wasn't available. Saul Panzer had come at nine o'clock on the dot, and instead of going up to the plant rooms Wolfe had come down, put on his heavy overcoat and broad-brimmed beaver hat, and followed Saul out to the curb to climb into the Heron sedan. Of course he knew that the heater, if turned on full, could make the inside of the Heron like an oven, but he took the heavy coat because he distrusted all machines more complicated than a wheelbarrow. He would have been expecting to be stranded at some wild and lonely spot in the Long Island jungle even if I had been driving.

It took will power to fasten my mind on the Frank Odell caper, which was merely a stab in the dark blind-folded, ordered by Wolfe only because he preferred the second of the three alternatives. Where my mind wanted to be was on Long Island. In all my experience of Wolfe's arrangements of circumstances I had never known him to concoct anything as tricky as the program he was going to rope Lewis Hewitt in for, and I should have been there. Genius is fine for the ignition spark, but to get there someone has to see that the radiator doesn't leak and no tire is flat. I would have insisted on going if it hadn't been for Saul Panzer. Wolfe had said that Saul would sit in, and he is the one man I would turn any problem over to if I broke a leg.

I forced my mind onto Frank Odell. The obvious thing was to ring the New York State Parole Division and ask if they had him listed. But of course not on our phone. If the FBI knew that we were spending time and money on Odell after what Quayle had said about him, they would know it wasn't just prudence, that we thought there was actually a chance that he was involved, and that wouldn't do. I decided to play it absolutely safe. If some G-man reads this and thinks I'm overrating his outfit, he isn't inside far enough to know all the family secrets. I'm not inside at all, but I've been around a lot.

After going to the kitchen to tell Fritz I was leaving and to the hall for my coat and hat, I let myself out, walked to Tenth Avenue and on to the garage, got permission from Tom Halloran to use the phone, dialed the *Gazette* number, and got Lon Cohen. He was discreet. He didn't ask me how we were making out with

Mrs. Bruner and the FBI. He did ask if I knew where he could get a bottle of brandy.

"I might send you one someday," I said, "if you earn it. You can start now. About two years ago a man named Frank Odell was sent up for fraud. If he behaved himself and got a reduction he may be out and on the parole list. I've gone in for social work and I want to find him, quick, and rehabilitate him. You can get me, the sooner the better, at this number." I gave it to him. "I'm keeping my social work secret, so please don't mention it."

He said an hour should do it, and I went out to the floor to give motor vehicles a look. Wolfe buys a new one every year, thinking that reduces the risk of a collapse, which it doesn't, and he leaves the choice to me. I have been tempted to get a Rolls, but it would be a shame to ditch it after only a year. That day there was nothing on the floor I would have traded the Heron for. Tom and I were discussing the dashboard of a 1965 Lincoln when the phone rang and I went. It was Lon, and he had it. Frank Odell had been released in August and would be on parole until the end of February. He lived at 2553 Lamont Avenue, Bronx, and he had a job at a branch of the Driscoll Renting Agency at 4618 Grand Concourse. Lon said that a good way to start rehabilitating him would be to get him in a poker game, and I said I thought craps would be better.

I decided to take the subway instead of a taxi, not to save the client money, but because I thought it was about time to do something about tails. There had been two days and nights since the FBI had presumably got interested in us, and twenty-five hours since they had asked Perazzo to take our licenses, and I still had seen no sign that I had company. Of course I had dodged or hadn't looked. I now decided to look, but not while walking. I waited until I was at the Grand Central subway station and had boarded an uptown express.

If you think you have a tail on a subway train and want to spot him you keep moving while the train is under way, and at each station you stand close enough to a door so that you might get off. At a rush hour it's difficult, but it was ten-thirty in the morning and we were going uptown. I had him by the time we made the third stop—or rather, them. There were two. One was a chunky specimen, barely tall enough to meet the specifications, with big brown eyes that he didn't know how to handle, and the other was the Gregory Peck type except for his curly little ears. The game, just for the hell of it, was to spot them without their knowing I had, and when I got off at the 170th Street station I was pretty sure I had won it. Out on the sidewalk again, I ignored them.

Tailing on New York streets, if you know you have it and want to shake it and aren't a birdbrain, is a joke. There are a thousand dodges, and the tailee merely picks the one that fits the time and place. There on Tremont Avenue I moseyed along, glancing occasionally at my wristwatch and at the numbers on doors, until I saw an empty taxi coming. When it was thirty yards away I scooted between parked cars, flagged it, hopped in, told the hackie as I pulled the door shut, "Step on it," and saw Gregory Peck stare at me as we went by. The other one was across the street. We did seven blocks before a red light stopped us, so that was that. I admit I had kept an eye on the rear. I gave the driver the Grand Concourse address, and the light changed, and we rolled.

Some realty agency branch offices are upstairs, but that one was on the ground floor of an apartment building, of course one of the buildings it serviced. I entered. It was small, two desks and a table and a filing cabinet. A beautiful young lady with enough black hair for a Beatle was at the nearest desk, and when she smiled at me and asked if she could help me I had to take a breath to keep my head from swimming. They should stay home during business hours. I told her I would like to see Mr. Odell, and she turned her beautiful head and nodded to the rear.

He was at the other desk. I had waited to see him before deciding on the approach, and one look was enough. Some men, after a hitch in the jug, even a short one, have got a permanent wilt, but not him. In size he was a peanut, but an elegant peanut. Fair-skinned and fair-haired, he was more than fair-dressed. His pin-stripe gray suit had set him, or somebody, back at least two Cs.

He left his chair to come, said he was Frank Odell, and offered a hand. It would have been simpler if he had had a room to himself; possibly she didn't know she was cooped up with a jailbird. I said I was Archie Goodwin, got out my case, and handed him a card. He gave it a good look, stuck it in his pocket, and said, "My goodness, I should have recognized you. From your picture in the paper."

My picture hadn't been in the paper for fourteen months, and he had been behind bars, but I didn't make an issue of it. "I'm beginning to show my years," I told him. "Can you give me a few minutes? Nero

Wolfe has taken on a little job involving a man named
Morris Althaus and he thinks you might be able to
furnish some information."

He didn't bat an eye. No wilt. He merely said,
"That's the man that was murdered."

"Right. Of course the police have been around about
that. Routine. This is just a private investigation on a
side issue."

"If you mean the police have been *here,* they
haven't. We might as well sit down." He moved to his
desk, and I followed and took a chair at its end. "What's
the side issue?" he asked.

"It's a little complicated. It's about some research
he was doing at the time he was killed. You may know
something about it if you saw him during that period
—say the month of November, last November. Did you
see him around then?"

"No, the last time I saw him was two years ago. In a
courtroom. When some people that I thought were
friends of mine were making me the goat. Why would
the police be seeing *me?*"

"Oh, in a murder case they can't crack they see
everybody." I waved it away. "What you say about
being made the goat, that's interesting. It might have
some bearing on what we want to know, whether
Althaus was in the habit of doctoring his stuff. Was
he one of the friends who made you the goat?"

"My goodness, no. He wasn't a friend. I only met
him twice, while he was doing that piece, or getting
ready to. He was looking for bigger fish. I was just a
hustler, working for Bruner Realty."

"Bruner Realty?" I wrinkled my brow. "I don't remember that name in connection with the case. Of

course I'm not any too familiar with it. Then it was your friends in Bruner Realty who made you the goat?"

He smiled. "You certainly are *not* familiar with it. It was some outside deals that I had a hand in. That all came out at the trial. The Bruner people were very nice about it, *very* nice. The vice-president even arranged for me to see Mrs. Bruner herself. That was the second time I saw Althaus, in her office at her house. She was nice too. She believed what I told her. She even paid my lawyer, part of it. You see, she realized that I had got mixed up in a shady deal, but I explained to her that I hadn't known what I was getting into, and she didn't want a man who was working for her company to get a bum deal. I call that *nice*."

"So do I. I'm surprised you didn't go back to Bruner Realty when you got—when you could."

"They didn't want me."

"That wasn't very nice, was it?"

"Well, it's the philosophy of it. After all, I had been convicted. The president of the company is a pretty tough man. I could have gone to Mrs. Bruner, but I have a certain amount of pride, and I heard about this opening with Driscoll." He smiled. "I'm not licked, far from it. There's plenty of opportunity in this business, and I'm still young." He opened a drawer. "You gave me a card, I'll give you one."

He gave me about a dozen, not one, and some information about the Driscoll Renting Agency. They had nine offices in three boroughs and handled over a hundred buildings, and they gave the finest service in the metropolitan area. I received a strong impression that Driscoll was *nice*. I listened to enough of it to be polite, and thanked him, and on the way out I took the liberty of exchanging glances with the beautiful young lady, and she smiled at me. That was certainly a nice place.

I strolled down the Grand Concourse in the winter sunshine, cooling off; I hadn't been invited to remove my coat. I was listing the items of the coincidence:

1. Mrs. Bruner had distributed copies of that book.
2. Morris Althaus had been collecting material for a piece on the FBI.
3. G-men had killed Althaus, or at least had been in his apartment about the time he was killed.
4. Althaus had met Mrs. Bruner. He had been in her house.
5. A man who had worked for Mrs. Bruner's firm had been jailed (made the goat?) as a result of a piece Althaus had written.

That was no coincidence; it was cause and effect in a hell of a mess. I started to sort it out but soon found that there were so many combinations and possibilities that you could even come up with the notion that Mrs. Bruner had shot Althaus, which wouldn't do, since she was the client. The one conclusion was that there *was* a needle in *this* haystack, and it had to be found. Wolfe had stolen another base. He had merely asked Yarmack if the articles Althaus had written for *Tick-Tock* were innocuous, and had merely told me to find Odell because he couldn't think of anything sensible for me, and here was this.

I couldn't have called Wolfe even if he had been at home, and I decided not to ring him at Hewitt's. Not only does a place like that have a dozen or more extensions, but also G-men had probably followed him there, since Saul had been told to ignore tails, and tapping a line in the country was a cinch for them. I happen to know that they once— But I'll skip it.

But I was not going to go home and sit on it until he got back. I found a phone booth, dialed Mrs. Bruner's number and got her, and asked if she could meet me at Rusterman's at twelve-thirty for lunch. She said she could. I rang Rusterman's and got Felix and asked if I could have the soundproofed room upstairs, the small one. He said I could. I went out and got a taxi.

Rusterman's has lost some of the standing it had when Marko Vukcic was alive. Wolfe is no longer the trustee, but he still goes there about once a month and Felix comes to the old brownstone now and then for advice. When Wolfe goes, taking Fritz and me, we eat in the small room upstairs, and we always start with the queen of soups, Germiny à l'Oseille. So I knew that room well. Felix was there with me, being sociable, when Mrs. Bruner came, only ten minutes late.

She wanted a double dry martini with onion. You never know; I would have guessed hers would be sherry or Dubonnet, and certainly not the onion. When it came she took three healthy sips in a row, looked to see that the waiter had closed the door, and said, "Of course I didn't ask you on the phone. Something has happened?"

I had a martini to keep her company, without the onion. I took a sip and said, "Nothing big. Mr. Wolfe has broken two rules today. He skipped his morning session in the plant rooms, and he left the house on business—your business. He is out on Long Island seeing a man. That could develop into something, but don't hold your breath. As for me, I just made a trip to the Bronx to see a man named Frank Odell. He used to work for you—Bruner Realty. Didn't he?"

"Odell?"

"Yes."

She frowned. "I don't— Oh, of course. Odell, that's the little man who had all that trouble. But he—isn't he in prison?"

"He was. He was paroled out a few months ago."

She was still frowning. "But why on earth were you seeing him?"

"It's a long story, Mrs. Bruner." I took a sip. "Mr. Wolfe decided to try getting a start by checking a little on FBI activities in and around New York. Among other things, we learned that last fall a man named Morris Althaus had been gathering material for a piece on the FBI for a magazine, and seven weeks ago he was murdered. That was worth looking into, and we did some checking on him. We learned that he did a piece called 'The Realty Racket' a couple of years ago, and as a result a man named Frank Odell had got a jail sentence for fraud. Mr. Wolfe had me look him up, and I located him and went to see him and learned that he had worked for your firm. So I thought I ought to ask you about it."

She had put the glass on the table. "But what is there to ask me?"

"Just questions. For instance, about Morris Althaus. How well did you know him?"

"I didn't know him at all."

"He came at least once to your house—your office. According to Odell."

She nodded. "That's right, he did. I remembered that when I read about him—the murder." Her chin was up. "I don't like your tone, Mr. Goodwin. Are you intimating that I have concealed something?"

"Yes, Mrs. Bruner, I am. That you *may* have. We might as well clear it up before lunch instead of after. You have hired Mr. Wolfe to do a job that's as close to impossible as a job can get. The least you can do is tell us everything that could conceivably have a bearing on it. The fact that you had known Morris Althaus, at least you had met him, naturally suggests questions. Did you know he was working at a piece on the FBI? Let me finish. Did you know or suspect that the FBI was involved in his murder? Was that why you sent those books? Was that why you came to Nero Wolfe? Just stay in the buggy. We simply have to know everything you know, that's all."

She did all right. A woman who can toss you a check for a hundred grand without blinking hasn't had much practice listening to reason from a hireling, but she managed it. She didn't count ten, at least not audibly, but she picked up her glass and drank, gave me a straight look, put the glass down, and spoke. "I didn't 'conceal' anything. It just didn't occur to me to mention Morris Althaus. Or perhaps it did occur to me while I was thinking about it, but not while I was talking to Mr. Wolfe. Because it was just—I didn't really *know* anything. I don't know anything now. I had read about the murder and remembered that I had met him, but the only connection it had with the FBI was what Miss Dacos, my secretary, had told me, and that was just a girl talking. She didn't really *know* anything either. It had nothing to do with my sending the books. I sent them because I had read it, and I thought it was important for important people to read it. Does that answer your questions?"

"Pretty well, but it raises another one. Just keep in mind that I'm working on your job. What had Miss Dacos told you?"

"Nothing but talk. She lived at the same address, she still does. Her—"

"What same address?"

"The same as that man, Morris Althaus. In the Village. Her apartment is on the second floor, below his. She was out that evening, and soon after—"

"The night he was killed?"

"Yes. Stop interrupting me. Soon after she returned to her apartment she heard footsteps outside, people going down the stairs, and she was curious about who it might be. She went to the window and looked out and saw three men leave the house and walk to the corner, and she thought they were FBI men. The only reason she had for thinking they were FBI men was that they looked like it; she said they were 'the type.' As I said, she didn't *know* anything, and I didn't know there was any connection between Morris Althaus and the FBI. You asked if I knew he was working on a piece on the FBI. No, not until you told me. I resent your suggestion that I concealed something." She looked at her wristwatch. "It's after one o'clock, and I have an appointment at half past two, a committee meeting that I must be on time for."

I pushed a button, two shorts, on a slab on the table, and begged her pardon for asking her to lunch and then starving her. In a couple of minutes Pierre came with the lobster bisque, and I told him to bring the squabs in ten minutes without waiting for a ring.

There was a little question of etiquette. As a matter
of business it would have been proper to tell her that
neither Nero Wolfe nor I was ever allowed to pay for
anything we or our guests ate at Rusterman's, so it
wouldn't be an item on the expense account, but such
a remark didn't seem to fit with Squabs *à la Moscovite,*
Mushrooms *Polonaise, Salade Béatrice,* and *Soufflé
Armenonville.* I vetoed it. I didn't resume on Miss
Dacos, but our only known common interest was the
FBI. I learned that she had received 607 letters thank-
ing her for the book, most of them just a polite sentence or two; 184 disapproving letters, some pretty
strong; and 29 anonymous letters and cards calling
her names. I was surprised that it was only 29; out of
the 10,000 there must have been a couple of hundred
members of the John Birch Society and similar outfits.

With the coffee I returned to Miss Dacos, having
done some calculating. If Wolfe left Hewitt's at four
o'clock he would get back around five-thirty, but he
might leave later, say five, and arrive at six-thirty, in
need of refreshment after the dangerous trip in the
dark of night surrounded by thousands of treacherous
machines. It would have to be after dinner. When
Pierre left after serving coffee I told Mrs. Bruner, "Of
course Mr. Wolfe will have to see Miss Dacos. She may
know nothing, as you say, but he'll have to satisfy himself on that. Will you tell her to be here at nine o'clock
this evening? In this room. Our office may be bugged."

"But I told you it was just a girl talking."

I said she was probably right, but one of Wolfe's
specialties was prying something useful out of people
who just talk, and when she finished her coffee I took

her to Felix's office in the rear, and she got Miss Dacos on the phone and arranged it.

After I escorted her downstairs and into her car I went back up and had another cup of coffee. I would wait to call Wolfe until I was sure they had finished lunch. I sat and looked things over. I had slipped up on one point; I hadn't asked if Miss Dacos had been present when Morris Althaus and Frank Odell had talked with Mrs. Bruner in her office. Of course Miss Dacos could tell us, but it was the kind of detail that Wolfe expects me to cover, and I expect me to too. How good a guess was it that it was Sarah Dacos who had told the cops about the three men? Not good at all, unless she had dressed it up or down either for the cops or for Mrs. Bruner. She couldn't see them go to a car around the corner, and get the license number, from the window of Number 63. Then we could be getting corroboration, but for the first alternative, that the FBI killed him, not for the one we preferred. But so what, since it was no longer futile, according to Wolfe's program.

I remembered how, crossing Washington Square yesterday on my sightseeing trip, I had thought it was coincidence that Arbor Street was in the Village and Sarah Dacos lived in the Village. Now it might be more than coincidence; it might be some more cause and effect.

At three o'clock I went to Felix's office and called Lewis Hewitt's number. There's something wrong with the way the people in that palace handle phone calls. It took a good four minutes, but finally Wolfe's voice came.

"Yes, Archie?"

"Yes and no," I said, "but more yes than no. I'm at
Rusterman's. Mrs. Bruner and I had lunch here. If you
get here before six-thirty I can report before dinner.
We might as well eat here because someone is coming
at nine o'clock to discuss things."

"Coming there?"

"Yes, sir."

"Why? Why not the office?"

"It will be better here. Unless you want an attractive
young woman practically sitting on your lap for a couple of hours with the radio going."

"What young woman?"

"Sarah Dacos, Mrs. Bruner's secretary. I'll report
when you come."

"*If* I come. Very well." He hung up.

I dialed the number I knew best and told Fritz we
would dine at Rusterman's and he would have to leave
the venison chops in the marinade until tomorrow.
Then I got Mrs. David Althaus's number from the book
and dialed it, but by the time she got on I had decided
not to ask her on the phone. All I wanted to know was
if she had ever heard her son mention a girl named
Sarah Dacos, but I had three hours to kill, so I might
as well take a walk. I asked if she would let me in if I
came around four-thirty, and she said yes. On the
way out I told Felix that Wolfe and I would be there
for dinner.

9

I was back in the soundproofed room, on my fanny with my legs stretched out and my eyes focused on my toes, going over the mess for the tenth time, when Wolfe arrived at twenty minutes to seven, ushered in by Felix. Knowing that was the busiest time of day downstairs for Felix, I shooed him out and took Wolfe's coat and hung it up and said I hoped he had had an interesting trip.

He growled and went and sat in the armchair which Marko Vukcic had bought years ago for his friend Nero's exclusive use. Between Wolfe's visits it is kept in the room that was Marko's personal den. "I have decided," he said, "that every man alive today is half idiot and half hero. Only heroes could survive in the maelstrom, and only idiots would want to."

"It's tough in spots," I conceded, "but you'll feel better after you eat. Felix has woodcock."

"I know he has." He glared. "You enjoy it."

"I have up to now. Now, I'm not so sure. How about Hewitt?"

"Confound it, he enjoys it too. Everything is arranged. Saul was very helpful, as he always is. Satisfactory."

I went and took a chair. "My report may not be satisfactory, but it has its points. To begin at the end, Mrs. Althaus says that she never heard her son mention Sarah Dacos."

"Why should he?"

"That's one of the points. Cause and effect."

I reported, the conversations in full and the actions in detail, including the frolic with the G-men. It had been our first actual contact with the enemy, and I thought he should know how we had handled ourselves. That armchair wasn't as good as his in the office for leaning back and closing his eyes, but it would do, and it was almost like home. When I finished he didn't move a muscle, not even opening an eye. I sat through three minutes of complete silence and then spoke.

"I understand, of course, that all that bored you—if you bothered to listen. You don't give a damn who killed Morris Althaus. All you're interested in is this cocky shenanigan you're cooking up, and to hell with who murdered whom. I appreciate your not snoring. A sensitive man like me."

His eyes opened. "Pfui. I can say satisfactory, and I do. Satisfactory. But you could have proceeded. You could have had that woman here this afternoon instead of this evening."

I nodded. "You're not only bored, your connections are jammed. You said we prefer by far the second alternative, so we certainly want to know if there is any chance of getting it. Sarah Dacos was there in the house, if not when he was shot, soon after. It's possible she can settle it, one way or the other. If you want—"

The door opened, and Pierre entered with a loaded tray. I glanced at my watch: 7:15. So he had told Felix a quarter past seven; by gum, he was hanging on to one rule at least, and he would certainly hang on to another one, no business talk at the table. He got up and left the room to wash his hands. By the time he got back Pierre had the mussels served and was waiting to hold his chair. He sat, forked a mussel to his mouth, used his tongue and teeth on it, swallowed, nodded, and said, "Mr. Hewitt has bloomed four crosses between *Miltonia sanderae* and *Odontoglossum pyramus*. One of them is worth naming."

So they had found time to visit the orchid house.

Around half past eight Felix came and asked if he could have a minute to discuss the problem of shipping *langoustes* from France by air. It developed that what he really wanted was Wolfe's approval of frozen *langoustes*, and of course he didn't get it. But he was stubborn, and they were still at it when Pierre ushered Sarah Dacos in. She was right on time. As I took her coat she accepted my offer of coffee, so I put her in a chair at the table and waited until Felix had gone to tell Wolfe her name.

He sizes a man up, but not a woman, because of his conviction that any opinion formed of any woman is sure to be wrong. He looked at Sarah Dacos, of course, since he was to talk to her. He told her that he supposed Mrs. Bruner had told her of her conversation with me.

She wasn't as chipper as she had been in her office; the hazel eyes weren't so lively. Mrs. Bruner had said that she had just talked; perhaps, sent to tell Nero Wolfe about it, she was feeling that she had just talked too much. She said yes, Mrs. Bruner had told her.

Wolfe blinked at her. The light there wasn't like the office, and besides, his eyes had had a hard day. "My interest is centered on Morris Althaus," he said. "Did you know him well?"

She shook her head. "Not really, no."

"You lived under the same roof."

"Well . . . that doesn't mean anything in New York, you know that. I moved there about a year ago, and when we met in the hall one day we realized we had met before—at Mrs. Bruner's office, the day he was there with that man, Odell. After that we had dinner together sometimes—maybe twice a month."

"It didn't progress to intimacy."

"No. No matter how you define 'intimacy.' We weren't intimate."

"Then that's settled and we can get to the point. The evening of Friday, November twentieth. Did you dine with Mr. Althaus that evening?"

"No."

"But you were out?"

"Yes, I went to a lecture at the New School."

"Alone?"

She smiled. "You're like Mr. Goodwin, you want to prove you're a detective. Yes, I was alone. The lecture was on photography. I'm interested in photography."

"What time did you get back to your apartment?"

"A little before eleven o'clock. About ten minutes

to eleven. I was going to listen to the eleven-o'clock news."

"And then? Be as precise as possible."

"There isn't much to be precise about. I went in and went upstairs—it's one flight—and into my apartment. I took my coat off and got a drink of water, and I was starting to undress when I heard footsteps out on the stairs. It sounded as if they were trying to be quiet, and I was curious. There are only four floors, and the woman on the top floor was away—she had gone to Florida. I went to the window and opened it enough to put my head out, and three men came out and turned left, and they turned at the corner, walking fast." She gestured. "That was all."

"Did they, one or more of them, hear you open the window and look up?"

"No. I had the window open before they came out."

"Did they speak?"

"No."

"Did you recognize them? Any of them?"

"No. Of course not."

"Not necessarily 'of course.' But you didn't."

"No."

"Could you identify them?"

"No. I didn't see their faces."

"Did you notice any peculiarities—size, manner of walking?"

"Well . . . no."

"You didn't?"

"No."

"So you went to bed."

"Yes."

"After you entered your apartment, before you heard

footsteps on the stairs, did you hear any sound above you, in Mr. Althaus's apartment?"

"I didn't notice any. I was moving around, taking my coat off and putting it away, and the water was running, getting it cold enough to drink. And his room had a thick carpet."

"You had been in it?"

She nodded. "A few times. Three or four times. For a drink before we went to dinner." She picked up her cup, and her hand was steady. I said her coffee was cold and offered to pour her some hot, but she said it was all right and drank. Wolfe poured himself some and took a sip.

"When and how," he asked her, "did you learn that Mr. Althaus had been killed?"

"In the morning. I don't work on Saturday and I sleep late. Irene, the cleaning woman, came and banged on my door. It was after nine o'clock."

"Then it was you who phoned the police?"

"Yes."

"Did you tell them of seeing the three men leave the house?"

"Yes."

"Did you tell them that you thought they were FBI men?"

"No. That hadn't—it was—I guess I was in shock. I had never seen a dead body before—except in a coffin."

"When did you tell Mrs. Bruner that you thought they were FBI men?"

Her lips moved, a moment of hesitation. "On Monday."

"Why did you think they were FBI men?"

"They *looked* like it. They looked young, and—well, sort of athletic, and the way they walked."

"You said there were no peculiarities."

"I know I did. It wasn't—I wouldn't call it *peculiarities.*" She bit her lip. "I knew you would ask me this. I think I ought to admit—I think the main reason I told her that was because I knew how she felt about the FBI, I had heard her talking about that book, and I thought she would like—I mean, that would agree with how she felt about them. I don't like to admit this, Mr. Wolfe, of course I don't. I know how it sounds. I hope you won't tell Mrs. Bruner."

"I'll tell her only if it suits a purpose." Wolfe picked up his cup, drank, put the cup down, and looked at me. "Archie?"

"Maybe one or two little points." I looked at her, and she looked back. The hazel eyes seemed darker when they were straight at you. "Of course," I said, "the cops have asked you about the last time you spoke with Althaus. When was it?"

"Three days before—before that Friday. Tuesday morning, in the hall, just a minute or two. Just by accident."

"Did he tell you he was doing a piece on the FBI?"

"No. He never talked to me about his work."

"When was the last time you were with him—for dinner, for anything?"

"I'm not sure about the date. It was about a month before, some day in October. We had dinner together."

"At a restaurant?"

"Yes. Jerry's Joint."

"Have you ever met Miss Marian Hinckley?"

"Hinckley? No."

"Or a man named Vincent Yarmack?"

"No."

"Or one named Timothy Quayle?"

"No."

"Did Althaus ever mention any of those names?"

"Not that I remember. He might have *mentioned* them."

I raised my brows at Wolfe. He regarded her for half a minute, grunted, and told her he doubted if she had supplied anything that would help, so the evening had probably been wasted. As he spoke I went and got her coat, and held it for her when she got up. Wolfe didn't leave his chair. He does sometimes rise when a woman comes or goes; he probably has some kind of a rule for it, but I have never been able to figure it out. She said I needn't bother to see her downstairs, but, wishing to show her that some private detectives have some manners, I went along. Down on the sidewalk, as the doorman waved a taxi up, she put her hand on my arm and said she would be *so* grateful if we didn't tell Mrs. Bruner, and I patted her shoulder. Patting a shoulder can be anything from an apology to a promise, and only the patter can say which.

When I got back to the room upstairs Wolfe was still in the armchair, with his fingers clasped at the peak of his middle mound. When I turned from shutting the door he growled, "Does she lie?"

I said certainly and went and sat.

"How the devil can you tell?"

"All right," I said, "to skip argument I'll concede that I am wise to attractive young women and you are not, since that's your line. But even you must know that she is not a big enough sap to give Mrs. Bruner that guff

about FBI men just because she thought she would like
to hear it. I doubt if she's a sap at all. But she did tell
Mrs. Bruner that, so she had a reason, and not just some
bull about how they walked. She had a real reason, God
knows what. One guess out of a dozen: When she went
in the house she heard noises, and went up another
flight and listened at Althaus's door, and heard something they said. I don't like it, because if it was something like that why didn't she tell the cops? I prefer
something she wouldn't want to spill. For instance, she
knew Althaus was working on the FBI. He had—"

"How did she know?"

"Oh, it *had* progressed to intimacy. That's the easiest
lie a woman can tell, they've been telling that one for
ten thousand years. Very convenient, there in the same
house, and he liked women and she is no hag. He had
told her. He had even told her they might call on him
uninvited when he wasn't home. So she—"

"She would have gone up to see if he was there."

"She did, after she saw the three men leaving, but the
door was locked and she had no key, and her knock or
ring wasn't answered. Anyway, I am only answering
your question does she lie. She does."

"Then we need the truth. Get it."

That was par. He does not believe that I can take a
girl to the Flamingo and dance a couple of hours and
end up with all her deepest secrets, but he pretends he
does because he thinks it makes me try harder.

"I'll consider it," I said. "I'll sleep on it—on the couch.
May I change the subject? Last night you asked me if I
could contrive any maneuver that would help to make
Wragg believe that one of his men killed Althaus, and I
said I couldn't. But I have. They have an open tail on

Sarah Dacos, so they know she was here, and almost
certainly they know you are. Also they know she lives
at Sixty-three Arbor Street, and they do not know what
she saw or heard that night. Therefore they don't know
what she might have told you here tonight, but they'll
assume it was something about *that* night. That should
help."

"Possibly. Satisfactory."

"Yeah. But. If we take a taxi, now, to Cramer's home
and spend an hour with him, they will absolutely assume that we have got something hot regarding his unsolved homicide, and that we got it from Sarah Dacos.
That *would* help."

He shook his head. "You gave Mr. Cramer our word
of honor."

"Only about his seeing me and telling me. We go to
him because in trying to dig up something on the FBI
we got interested in Morris Althaus because he was
working on them, and he was murdered, and Sarah
Dacos tells us something about the murder that we
think Cramer should know. Our word of honor is good
as gold."

"What time is it?"

I looked. "Three minutes to ten."

"Mr. Cramer would be in bed, and we have nothing
for him."

"The hell we haven't. We have someone who had
some reason for thinking they were G-men and is saving it. That will be pie for Cramer."

"No. It's our pie. We'll give Mr. Cramer Miss Dacos
only when we have her ourselves, if at all." He pushed
his chair back. "Get it out of her. Tomorrow. I'm tired.
We're going home and to bed."

10

At 10:35 Saturday morning I used a key on the door of
63 Arbor Street, ascended two flights of wooden stairs,
used another key, and entered the apartment that had
been Morris Althaus's.

I was following my own approach to the problem of
getting it out of Sarah Dacos. I admit it was roundabout, especially in view of the fact that time was short,
but it was a better stab at getting results than persuad-
ing her to go to the Flamingo for an evening of dancing. The fact that time was short had been made
publicly evident by an item on the twenty-eighth page
of the morning paper, which I had read at my breakfast
table in the kitchen. It was headlined FINGERS CROSSED?
and said:

> The members of the Ten for Aristology, one of the
> most exclusive of New York's gourmet groups, evi-

dently do not believe that history repeats itself. Lewis Hewitt, capitalist, socialite, orchid fancier, and aristologist, will entertain the group at dinner at his home at North Cove, Long Island, on Thursday evening, January 14. The menu will be chosen by Nero Wolfe, the well-known private investigator, and the food will be prepared by Fritz Brenner, Mr. Wolfe's chef. Mr. Wolfe and Archie Goodwin, his confidential assistant, will be present as guests.

That arrangement arouses memory of another occasion when Mr. Brenner cooked a dinner for the Ten for Aristology, and Mr. Wolfe and Mr. Goodwin were guests, at the home of Benjamin Schriver, the shipping magnate. It occurred on April 1, 1958, and one of the Ten, Vincent Pyle, head of a Wall Street brokerage firm, was poisoned with arsenic in his portion of the first course, served to him by Carol Annis, who was subsequently convicted of first-degree murder.

Yesterday a *Times* reporter, remembering that former occasion, telephoned Mr. Hewitt and asked him if any of the Ten for Aristology (aristology means science of dining) had shown any reluctance to attend the affair next Thursday, and Mr. Hewitt said no. When the reporter asked him if he would keep his fingers crossed he said, "How can I? I couldn't handle my knife and fork."

It will certainly be an excellent meal.

Setting the date definitely, Thursday the fourteenth, was the detail I had been hottest about when discussing it with Wolfe Thursday night. I said it should be left open, that the item in the paper could say something like "some evening this month." Wolfe said that Hewitt, when phoning his fellow aristologists, would have to name a date. I said he could tell them it would

have to be indefinite because it would depend on when
Fritz could get something shipped by air from France.
Gourmets love things shipped by air from France. But
Wolfe had insisted, and now we were stuck with it,
only five days to go.

So I hadn't liked the roundabout approach to Sarah
Dacos, but it was obviously the best bet, and right after breakfast I had phoned Mrs. Althaus to ask if she
could give me ten minutes. She had said yes, and I had
gone, of course ignoring the tail problem. The more
they saw me working the Althaus angle, the better. I
told her there had been some developments which we
would tell her about when we had figured them out,
and it might help if she would let me take a look at
everything that had been in her son's apartment, at
least what was left of it. She said everything was left.
The lease had nearly a year to go, and they hadn't
tried to sublet. They hadn't removed anything, and as
far as she knew the police hadn't either; they hadn't
asked for permission to. I promised to take nothing
without her permission if she would let me go and have
a look, and she went and got the keys without phoning
the lawyer or even her husband. Perhaps I appeal more
to middle-aged women than to young ones, but don't
try to tell Wolfe that.

So at 10:35 Saturday morning I entered the apartment of the late Morris Althaus, shut the door, and sent
my eyes around. It wasn't bad at all if you ignored the
pictures. As Sarah Dacos had said, the wall-to-wall carpet was thick. There was a big couch with a coffee
table in front of it, a good sitting chair near a lamp,
four other chairs, a small table with a metal object on
it that might have been created by some kid handy

with tools out of junk stuff he found in the garage, a large desk with nothing much on it besides a telephone, and a typewriter on a stand. Most of one wall had bookshelves, full, nearly to the ceiling. The less said about the pictures on the other walls the better. They would have been fine for a guessing game—have a party and everybody guesses what they are—if you could find someone who knew the answers.

I put my hat and coat on the couch and toured. Two closets in the living room. There was a bathroom, a small kitchen, and a bedroom with a single bed, a chest of drawers, a dresser, two chairs, and a closet full of clothes. On the dresser were framed photographs of his father and mother, so he hadn't resigned from the family, only from Peggy Pilgrim. I returned to the living room and started looking. With the tan drapes drawn it was dim, and I turned the lights on. The dust was thick on everything, but I was there legally and properly, so I didn't bother to put gloves on.

Of course I didn't expect to find anything obvious, pointing straight at anyone or anything in particular, since the cops had been through it, but they had had no one specifically in mind, and I did have: Sarah Dacos. No doubt you would like very much to have a complete inventory of everything in the place, especially the contents of the drawers and closets, but it would take too much space. I mention only one item, the 384 pages of the unfinished novel. I read a page and a half of it. To read it through to see if there was a girl in it who reminded me of Sarah Dacos would have taken all day.

The only other item I mention was in the bottom drawer of the chest in the bedroom. Along with a lot of other miscellaneous articles there were a dozen or so photographs. There was none of Sarah Dacos, but there was one of Althaus, lying on his side on the couch in the living room, with nothing on but his skin. I hadn't seen him naked before, since in the pictures of him in the *Gazette* file he had been decent. He had been in pretty good shape, muscles visible and belly flat, but the back of the photograph was more interesting than the front. Someone had written a poem on it, or part of one. I have since been allowed to reproduce it, so I can show it here:

Bold Lover, ever, ever shalt thou kiss,
And won the willing goal, and never leave;
She will not fade, and thou shalt have thy bliss,
Forever wilt thou love, and she be fair!

I haven't read all the poetry in the world, but Lily Rowan has a shelf of it and on certain occasions wants me to read some aloud to her, and I was pretty sure I had read that, but there was something wrong with it. I tried to place it but couldn't. Anyway, the point was, who had written it? Not Althaus; I had seen his hand on various items. Sarah Dacos? If so, I had something. I had plenty. I put it on top of the chest and spent another hour looking, but drew a blank.

I had promised Mrs. Althaus I would take nothing without her permission, but I was tempted. I could take the photograph, not out of the house, but just one flight down, knock at Sarah Dacos's door, and if she was there, as she might be on a Saturday, display it and ask her, "Did you write that?" It was a real temptation, so quick and direct. But it was too damned direct. I would have to stick to the roundabout. I left the apartment and the house, found a phone booth, dialed Mrs. Bruner's number and got her, and told her I wanted to come and ask her something. She said she would be there until one o'clock. It was only twenty past twelve. I went out and got a taxi.

She was in her office, at her desk with some papers, expecting me. She asked if Miss Dacos had come as arranged, saying she had rather expected her to phone, but she hadn't. I said yes, she had come, and had been very cooperative. I emphasized the "very," since it was possible that the room was bugged. Then I sat, leaned forward to her, and whispered, "Do you mind if we whisper?"

She frowned. "It is so ridiculous!"

"Yes," I whispered, "but it's safe. You don't need to say much. I only want a sample of Miss Dacos's handwriting. Anything—a memo, a note to you. I know this seems even more ridiculous, but it isn't. Don't ask me to explain because I can't. I'm following instructions. Either you trust Mr. Wolfe to do the job and do it right or you don't."

"But why on earth—" she began, but I showed her a palm.

"If you don't want to whisper," I whispered, "just give me what I asked for and I'll go."

When I left the house five minutes later, with two samples of Sarah Dacos's hand in my pocket—a nine-word entry on a sheet from a desk calendar and a six-line memo to Mrs. Bruner—I was feeling that middle-aged women are the backbone of the country. She hadn't whispered a word. She had fished in a drawer and got the memo and torn the sheet from the calendar, handed them to me, said, a little louder than usual,

"Let me know when there is something I *should* know," and picked up one of the papers. What a client.

In the taxi back downtown I inspected the samples, and I was already ninety-per-cent sure when I mounted the two flights at 63 Arbor Street. I went to the bedroom for the photograph, got comfortable in the good sitting chair under the lamp in the living room, and compared. I am not a handwriting expert, but it didn't need one. The person who had written the samples had written the poetry on the back of the photograph. Probably she had also taken the photograph, but that didn't matter. I formed a conclusion. I concluded that Sarah Dacos's memory had failed her when she said that it had not progressed to intimacy.

The immediate question was, should I phone Mrs. Althaus for permission to take the photograph, or should I leave it? I decided that leaving it would be too risky; Sarah might get in somehow and find it and take it. I got a sheet of typewriter paper from the desk and folded it, and inserted the photograph. It was almost too wide for my breast pocket, but I eased it in. I looked around a little, from habit, to be sure things were as I had found them, and left with my loot. As I passed the door of Sarah Dacos's apartment on the way down I threw it a kiss. Then it occurred to me that it rated more than a kiss, and I went and took a look at the lock. It was the same make as the one on Althaus's door, a Bermatt, nothing special.

At the same booth where I had phoned Mrs. Bruner I rang Mrs. Althaus's number, got her, told her I had left everything in order in the apartment, and asked if she wanted the keys returned immediately. She said at my convenience, no hurry.

"By the way," I said, "I'm taking one item, if you don't mind—a photograph of a man that was in a drawer. I want to see if someone recognizes it. All right?"

She said I was very mysterious, but yes, I could take it. I would have liked to tell her what I thought of middle-aged women but decided we weren't intimate enough. I dialed another number, told the woman who answered, whose name was Mimi, that I would like to speak to Miss Rowan, and in a moment the familiar voice came.

"Lunch in ten minutes. Come and get it."

"You're too young for me. I've decided women under fifty are—what are they?"

"Well, jejune's a good word."

"Too many Js. I'll think of one and tell you this evening. Two things. One, I have to be home at midnight. I'm sleeping in the office and— I'll explain when I see you."

"Good Lord, has he rented your room?"

"As a matter of fact, he has, for one night. I won't explain that. Hold it a second." I transferred the receiver to my right hand and used the left to slip the photograph from my pocket. "Here's some poetry. Listen." I read it, with feeling. "Do you recognize it?"

"Certainly. So do you."

"No I don't, but it seems familiar."

"It should. Where did you get it?"

"I'll tell you someday. What is it?"

"It's a take-off of the last four lines of the second stanza of Keats's 'Ode on a Grecian Urn.' It's sort of clever, but no one should monkey with Keats. Escamillo, you're a pretty good detective and you dance like an angel, and you have other outstanding qualities, but you will never be a highbrow. Come and read Keats to me."

I told her she was too jejune, hung up, slipped the photograph back in my pocket, and went out and took my fifth taxi in five hours. The client could afford it.

It was five minutes to two when I put my hat and coat on the rack in the hall, went to the door of the dining room, told Wolfe, who was at the table, that it looked and felt like snow, and proceeded to the kitchen. I don't join Wolfe when I arrive in the middle of a meal; we agree that for one man to hurry with meat or fish while the other dawdles with pastry or cheese is bad for the atmosphere. Fritz put things on my break-fast table and brought what was left of the baked blue-fish, and I asked him how he was getting on with the menu for next Thursday's blowout.

"I'm not discussing that," he said. "I am not discussing anything, Archie. He was in my room for more than an hour before lunch, talking with the television on loud. If it is so dangerous I will not talk at all."

I told him we should be back to normal by the time the shad roe started coming, and he threw up his hands and said good God in French.

When I finished and went to the office Wolfe was standing over by the globe, turning it and scowling at it. The man who gave him that globe, the biggest one I have ever seen, couldn't have known what a big help it would be. Whenever a situation gets so ticklish that he wishes he were somewhere else, he can walk over to the globe and pick spots to go to. Wonderful. As I entered he asked if I had anything, and when I nodded he went to his desk and I turned on the radio, took a yellow chair around near his elbow, and reported. It didn't take long, since there had been no conversation to speak of, just the action. I didn't mention the phone call to Lily Rowan because it had been purely personal.

Having read the poetry twice, he handed the photograph back to me and said she had an ear for meter.

"I told you she wasn't a sap," I said. "Pretty neat, doing that with the last four lines of the second stanza of Keats's 'Ode on a Grecian Urn.'"

His eyes narrowed at me. "How the deuce do you know that? You don't read Keats."

I shrugged. "Back in Ohio in my boyhood days. As you know, I have quite a memory. I don't brag about that, but I have a brag coming about this." I tapped the photograph. "We know why she lied. She's involved. Possibly not too deep; it could be that she merely didn't want to admit she was close with him, close enough for him to tell her about the FBI. Or possibly *very* deep. 'Ever, ever shalt thou kiss.' And 'Forever wilt thou love.' But he told her he was going to marry another girl, so she shot him, probably with his own gun. The second alternative, which we prefer by far. It would be hard to nail her. She might be able to prove she was at that lecture but not what time she left. Possibly she wasn't there at all. She spent the evening at Sixty-three Arbor Street, having it out with the bold lover, and she shot him before the G-men arrived. Does that appeal to you?"

"As conjecture, yes."

"Then I should look into the lecture question. She might have a tight alibi. According to Cramer, the G-men left about eleven o'clock, and of course they had combed the place, whether they killed him or not; they got the material he had gathered. So they arrived not later than ten-thirty, or even make it ten-forty. If she shot him she was out before they came. The New School is on Twelfth Street. If anyone saw her at the lecture as late as ten-twenty, or even a quarter past, she's clear. I'll start asking."

"No."

"No?"

"No. If they learned you were doing that, either by surveillance of you or through inadvertence, they would know we were seriously considering the possibility that that woman killed him, and that would be disastrous. We must maintain the illusion that we are convinced that a member of the Federal Bureau of Investigation killed Morris Althaus and that we are procuring evidence to establish it; otherwise our preparations for next Thursday evening will come to nothing. For protection of our flank we needed to know definitely if Miss Dacos was lying, and you have settled that: she was. Satisfactory. She lied to conceal the fact that she had compromised herself, and that satisfies us. Whether her involvement was merely a secret intimacy she doesn't want revealed, or was murder by her hand, is of no importance to us."

"Cramer would love to know that. After giving us the steer. I'll call him and tell him, to relieve his mind."

"Pfui. When we have relieved *our* minds by finishing the job we were hired to do we'll consider our obligation to him. If it seems feasible without excessive effort we'll expose the murderer for him. If it isn't a member of the FBI, as he expects and hopes, he won't thank us, but we'll owe him no apology."

"Then we forget the murder until after Thursday."

"Yes."

"That's just dandy. Agencies are closed today and tomorrow, so Hewitt can't start looking until Monday. I'll be at the Flamingo this evening if anything happens; for instance, if Hewitt calls to say he has decided that it's too much trouble and we have to find someone else. Tomorrow Miss Rowan is having a crowd in for Sunday lunch and dancing and I'll stay afterwards to help empty ashtrays. Any instructions for this afternoon?"

"Turn off the radio," he growled.

11

It bothered me for four days and four nights, from Saturday afternoon, when Wolfe said we would forget the murder, to Wednesday morning, when I did something about it on my own.

There were two aspects. First, if the conjecture about Sarah Dacos, or something like it, was actually a fact, I had removed evidence from the scene of a murder and was withholding it. Of course the cops had had their whack at it, they had certainly seen the photograph and had left it there, and Mrs. Althaus had given me the keys, but that was only a legal out. It was the second aspect that really bothered me. Cramer had saved our licenses for us, at least so far, and it was me, Archie Goodwin, he had invited to a conference and bought a carton of milk for and turned loose on a homicide. I have no objection to playing games with cops, sometimes you want to and sometimes you have to, but this was different. I owed Cramer something personally.

So it bothered me, but something else was bothering me still more, the act Wolfe was staging, the fanciest on record. Too much of it, nearly all of it, was entirely out of our control. For instance, when I called Hewitt from a booth Monday evening to ask how he had made out, and he said fine, he had got one actor at one agency and the other at another, and they would both come to his place Tuesday afternoon, and I asked if he had made sure that the one for me could drive a car and had a license, he said he had forgotten to ask, but everyone could drive a car! And that was absolutely vital and he knew it. He said he would find out right away; he had the actor's phone number. On some other details he was okay, like his phone call to our number Tuesday noon, as arranged. He told Wolfe he was extremely sorry, he apologized, but he would be able to include only twelve *Phalaenopsis Aphrodite* in the shipment instead of twenty, and no *Oncidium flexuosum* at all. He said he would do his best to get it off by noon Wednesday, so it should arrive by two o'clock. He handled that perfectly. He was also okay on the call he made Tuesday evening, to report on the supplies and arrangements for the dinner for the Ten for Aristology, but for him that was just routine, and anyway it was straight.

Fred Durkin and Orrie Cather were no worry because they had been left to Saul to handle, and if there was any snag he would let us know. How was up to him.

Off and on all day and evening Monday, and even some on Tuesday, Wolfe and I discussed a problem. It wasn't an argument; we just discussed it. Should I phone Wragg, the special agent in charge, arrange to meet him somewhere, tell him that Wolfe had got enough dope on the Althaus homicide to make it really tough and I wanted out, and offer to pass everything we had over to him for ten grand or twenty grand or fifty grand? The trouble was we didn't know him. It might make it next to certain that he would take the bait, but it might do just the opposite, make him smell a rat. Finally, late Tuesday morning, we crossed it off. It was too chancy, and time was too short.

At nine o'clock Wednesday morning, when I heard the elevator taking Wolfe up to the plant rooms, I took my second cup of breakfast coffee to the office, to sit and look at an idea that had been pecking at me off and on since Monday morning. There would be nothing for me until the truckload of orchids arrived at two o'clock; everything had been done that could be done as far as I knew, which wasn't very far. When I finished the coffee it was only nine-twenty, and Sarah Dacos probably didn't start the day at the Bruner office until nine-thirty or even ten. I went to the cabinet, unlocked the drawer where we keep assortments of keys, and made some selections. It wasn't complicated, since I knew the lock was a Bermatt. From another drawer I got a pair of rubber gloves.

At 9:35 I dialed the Bruner number, and it was answered. "Mrs. Bruner's office, good morning."

"Good morning. Miss Dacos?"

"Yes."

"This is Archie Goodwin. I may need to see Mrs. Bruner later today, and I'm calling to ask if she'll be available."

She said it depended on how late, Mrs. Bruner expected to be in the office from three-thirty to five-thirty, and I said I would call again if I needed to come.

So she was at her job. I would have to take a chance on the cleaning woman. I went to the kitchen to tell Fritz I was going out to make some phone calls, to the hall for my hat and coat, and out and to Ninth Avenue for a taxi.

For the street door at 63 Arbor Street I still had the key Mrs. Althaus had given me, so I was clean until I stood at Sarah Dacos's door and got out the collection of keys. When I had knocked twice, and pushed the button twice and heard the ring, with no response, I tried a key. The fourth one did it, smooth and easy. I put the gloves on, turned the knob, opened the door, crossed the sill, and shut the door, and I had broken and entered according to the statutes of the State of New York.

The layout was the same as upstairs, but the furniture was quite different. Rugs here and there instead of carpet, smaller couch smothered with pillows, no desk or typewriter, fewer chairs, about one-fourth as many books, five little pictures on the walls which the bold lover must have considered old hat. The drapes were drawn, and I turned the lights on, put my coat and hat on the couch, and went and opened a closet door.

There were two facts: the cleaning woman might come any minute, and I had no idea what I might find, if anything. The point was simply that there might be something that would help, no matter what was going to happen Thursday night, to square it with Cramer for that carton of milk. A fast once-over was called for, and

I spent only ten minutes on the living room and its two closets and then went to the bedroom.

I came mighty close to passing it by. The bedroom closet was crammed—clothes on hangers, shoe racks, luggage, cartons and hatboxes on two high shelves. The bag and two suitcases were packed with summer clothes, and I skipped the hatboxes; I would have given a finif of *my* money to know if the cleaning woman came Wednesdays. But ten minutes later, going through a drawerful of photographs one by one, I realized that it was dumb to skip the hatboxes and then waste time with a bunch of photographs which could tell me nothing I didn't already know, so I took a chair to the closet, mounted it, and got the boxes down. There were three. The first one contained three so-called hats and two bikinis. The second one held one big floppy hat. I lifted it out, and there on the bottom was a revolver. I gawked at it for five seconds, then took it out and inspected it. It was an S & W .38 and held one cartridge that had been fired and five that hadn't.

I stood with it in my hand. It was a hundred to one that it was the gun that Althaus had had a permit for, and it had fired the bullet that had gone through him, and Sarah Dacos had pulled the trigger. To hell with the one chance in a hundred. The question was what to do with it. If I took it, it would never be an acceptable exhibit in a murder trial, since I had got it illegally. If I left it there and went out to a phone booth and rang Cramer to tell him to get a warrant to search Sarah Dacos's apartment, the cops would get the gun all right, but if the FBI found out about it within thirty-six hours, as they easily might, the big act for Thursday night would be kaput. And of course if I left it in the hatbox and *didn't* phone Cramer, Sarah Dacos might decide that tonight would be a good time to take it and toss it in the river.

Since that left only one alternative, the only decision that had to be made was where to put it. I returned the hat to the box and the boxes to the shelf, put the chair back where it belonged, and looked around. No spot in the bedroom appealed to me, and I moved to the living room. It was now more than ever desirable not to be interrupted by a cleaning woman or anyone else. I went and examined the couch and found that underneath the cushion was a box spring, and underneath the spring was a plywood bottom. Good enough. If she got the hatbox down and found the gun gone, she certainly wouldn't suppose it had merely been moved to another spot in the apartment and start looking. I put it on the bottom under the spring, glanced around to see that things were as I had found them, grabbed my hat and coat, and got out of there in such a hurry that I almost appeared on the sidewalk wearing rubber gloves.

In the taxi I had to answer another question: did I or didn't I tell Wolfe? Why not wait until Thursday night had come and gone? The answer was really simple, but of course that's one thing we use our minds for, finding complicated reasons for dodging simple answers. By the time the cab stopped in front of the old brownstone my mind had run out of reasons and I was facing the fact that it wouldn't improve with age.

It was ten minutes past eleven, so Wolfe would be down from the plant rooms, but he wasn't in the office. There was noise in the kitchen, the radio going loud, and I went there. Wolfe was standing by the big table scowling at Fritz, who was bending over to sniff at a slab of smoked sturgeon. They didn't hear me enter, but Fritz saw me when he straightened up, and Wolfe turned and demanded, "Where have you been?"

I told him I had a report. He told Fritz to have the cutlets ready at a quarter past two, he wasn't going to wait longer than that, and headed for the office, and I followed. I turned the radio on. As I brought a yellow chair around I saw three screwdrivers on his desk pad —one from my desk drawer and two from the kitchen, and I had to grin. He had the tools ready, himself. As I sat I told him I had assumed that he would eat an early lunch. He said no, if a man has guests he should be at table with them.

"Then there's plenty of time," I said, "to discuss a brief report. With so much on your mind I could save it, but you'll like to know that I have clinched the alternative we prefer. I went for a walk and happened to pass Sixty-three Arbor Street, and I happened to have a key in my pocket that fitted the lock on Sarah Dacos's door, so I went in and looked around, and in a hatbox in a closet I found a revolver, an S and W thirty-eight. One cartridge had been fired. As you know, Cramer told me that Althaus had a permit for an S and W thirty-eight and it wasn't in his apartment, though there was a box of cartridges in a drawer. So she—"

"What did you do with it?"

"I moved it. It seemed out of place in a box with a lady's hat, so I put it under a box spring on a couch."

He took a deep breath, held it in a second, and let it out. "She shot him," he growled.

"Right. As I was saying when you interrupted."

"Will she find it?"

"No. If she misses it she won't even look. My understanding of attractive young women. She might lam. If she does I'll have a problem. If she's gone and I tell Cramer about the gun I'll be up a tree. If I don't tell him I'll lie awake nights."

He shut his eyes. In two moments he opened them. "You should have told me you were going."

"I should not. It was a personal errand in which a quart of milk was involved. Even if she stays put I'll have a problem, if tomorrow night is a turkey. If and if. Just now I wanted to ring Hewitt from a booth and ask him if the orchids are packed. Shall I?"

"No. He's busy. I believe guns can be identified?"

"Sure. Scientists can do it now even if the number has been filed off. And Cramer will have the number of the one Althaus had a permit for."

"Then there will be no problem. I must see about that sturgeon." He left his chair and headed for the door. Short of it he stopped and turned, said, "Satisfactory," and went. I shook my head and went on shaking it as I replaced the yellow chair. "There will be no problem," for God's sake. I thought if I had an ego that size I'd be the boss of the FBI, and then realized that that wasn't exactly the way to put it. I returned the keys and gloves to the cabinet, went to the kitchen to get a glass of milk, since lunch would be late, and to listen to them discuss sturgeon.

With a couple of hours to go, possibly more, after the milk was down I made the rounds—first two flights up to my room, to see that everything was in order for the guests who would occupy my bed. Fritz isn't supposed to touch my room; it's mine, including the responsibility. It was okay, except that the two pillows

I had got from the closet that morning weren't the same size, but that couldn't be helped. Then to the South Room, which is above Wolfe's, where two more guests would sleep on the twin beds. That visit was unnecessary, since Fritz never makes mistakes, but I had time to kill.

It got killed somehow.

I wasn't expecting them until two at the earliest, but I should have known better, since Saul was in charge. Wolfe was in the kitchen and I was in the front room, which adjoins the office, checking that blankets were on the sofa, when the doorbell rang and I glanced at my watch. Twenty to two, so it couldn't be the truck. But it was. Going to the hall, I saw a big bozo in a leather jacket on the stoop. When I opened the door he boomed at me, "Nero Wolfe? Orchids for you!"

I stepped out. At the curb was a big green truck with red lettering on its side: NORTH SHORE TRUCKING CORPORATION. Another big bozo was at its rear, opening the doors. I said fairly loud that it was pretty damn cold for orchids and I would come and help. By the time I got my coat on and went out they had a box on the edge at the back and were pulling it around. I happened to know its exact size—three feet wide, five feet long, and two feet high—because I had packed boxes exactly like it with orchid plants on their way to dealers or exhibitions. On its side it was marked:

FRAGILE   PERISHABLE
TROPICAL PLANTS
KEEP AS WARM AS POSSIBLE

I descended to the sidewalk, but they lifted it off and got the handles at the ends, obviously not needing

any help, even up the steps. Above, Wolfe had the
door open and they entered. The natural thing for me
was to stay and guard the truck, so I did. There were
five more boxes inside, all the same. One of the five
would be quite a load even for those two huskies, but
I didn't know which one. It proved to be the next to
the last. As they eased it down and took the handles
one of them said, "Jesus, these must be in lead pots,"
and the other one said, "Naw, gold." I wondered if
there was a G-man close enough to hear. They got it up
the stoop without a stumble, though it was close to
three hundred pounds, counting the box—or I hoped
it was. When they took the last one in I went along.
Wolfe signed a receipt, and I gave each of them two
bucks and got thanked and waited until they were on
the sidewalk to shut the door and bolt it.

The boxes were strung along the hall, the radio in the
office was on loud, and Wolfe was using a screwdriver
on the third box from the end. I asked him if he was
sure, and when he said yes, an X was chalked on it, I
got another screwdriver. There were only eight screws,
and in a couple of minutes we had them out. I lifted
the top off, and there was Saul Panzer, on his side with
his knees pulled up. I started to tilt the box, but Saul,
who is undersized except for his ears and nose, twisted
around and was on his knees and then his feet.

"Good afternoon," Wolfe said.

"Not very." Saul stretched. "I can talk?"

"Yes, with the radio."

He stretched again. "That was a ride. I hope they're
alive."

"I want to be sure," Wolfe said, "that I have their

names right. Mr. Hewitt gave them to Archie on the phone."

"Ashley Jarvis. That's you. Dale Kirby is Archie. We'd better get them out."

That was the first and only time I have ever heard men introduced while boxed.

"In a moment," Wolfe said. "You have given them a full explanation?"

"Yes, sir. They are not to speak, not a word, unless you ask them to—or Archie. They don't know who has bugged the house and is watching it, or why, but they have bought Hewitt's promise that they are in no danger and won't be. He gave them five hundred dollars apiece and you are to give them another five hundred. He also gave them the statements signed by you. I think they'll do." He lowered his voice a little. "Kirby is better than Jarvis, but they'll do."

"They know they are to stay in their room and keep away from windows?"

"Yes. Except when they are—uh—rehearsing."

"They have the proper clothes for Thursday evening?"

"In that box." Saul pointed. "Our things are in it too, including guns. Of course they'll wear your hat and coat, and Archie's."

Wolfe made a face. "Very well. Fred and Orrie first."

"They're marked." He took the screwdriver from Wolfe, went to the box with a circle chalked on it, told me, "Orrie's has a triangle," and started on a screw. I found the triangle and started on it. He had Fred out before I got Orrie because one of the screws had a bad head. They too had been told not to speak unless spoken to, and from the expressions on their faces when they

got upright I thought it was just as well. I raised my
brows at Saul and tapped my chest, and he pointed to
the box at the far end, and I went and started on it.

I realize that professional actors have had a lot of
practice saying only what they are supposed to say and
keeping their traps closed if that's what the script calls
for, but even so I had to hand it to Ashley Jarvis and
Dale Kirby. They had had a rough two hours or more
—especially Jarvis, who carried fully as many pounds as
Wolfe, and it wasn't quite as well distributed. We had
to ease the box over on its side before he could come
loose, and he stayed on the floor a good five minutes,
refusing offers of help, working his arms and legs, but
when he finally made it and was erect he turned to
Wolfe and bowed, a damn good bow. Kirby hadn't
bowed to me, but he hadn't said a word. While we
waited for Jarvis to get up he stood to one side doing
calisthenics, keeping time with the music on the radio.

I was agreeing with Saul, they'll do. Kirby was half
an inch shorter than me, but his build was just right.
Jarvis was exactly Wolfe's height. His shoulders
weren't quite as broad and his middle was a little far-
ther around, but with an overcoat on he would do fine.
The faces were only so-so, but it would be dark and no
G-man was going to get a close-up.

Wolfe returned the bow with a nod, said, "Come,
gentlemen," and entered the office. Instead of going to
his desk, he moved a yellow chair to the center of the
rug, which was thick enough to prevent noise, and went
for another one. I got a couple, and Saul and Fred and
Orrie each got one, and we all sat, in two circles, with
Wolfe and Jarvis and Kirby on the inside. But Wolfe
said, "The money, Archie," and I got up and went to

the safe for it—two wads with twenty-five twenties in each which were there waiting.

Wolfe's eyes went from Jarvis to Kirby and back. "Lunch is ready," he said, "but first a few points. That money is yours. Archie?"

I handed it to them, a wad to each. Jarvis merely glanced at it and stuck it in his side pocket. Kirby got a wallet from his breast pocket, put the bills in nice and neat, and replaced the wallet.

"Mr. Hewitt explained," Wolfe said, "that you would each receive one thousand dollars, and now you have. But having seen you emerge from those boxes, I feel that you have already earned the thousand. Amply. Therefore, if you perform the rest of it satisfactorily, I shall feel that you have earned another thousand, and you will receive it. Friday or Saturday."

Jarvis opened his mouth, remembered just in time, and shut it. He pointed to Kirby, tapped his own chest, and looked a question.

Wolfe nodded. "Two thousand. One to each of you. A little closer, Mr. Kirby. I must keep my voice down. You gentlemen will be here twenty-eight hours. During that period there must be no single sound which, if overheard, would disclose your presence in this house. Your room is two flights up. You will use the stairs, not the elevator. If you need something there will be a man in the hall outside. If you must communicate you will whisper. There are several dozen books in your room. If none of them is to your taste you may select one from these shelves. No radio or television; the house must not be a hubbub. You will need to observe closely the posture and manner of walking of Mr. Goodwin and me, and there will be opportunities. Not our voices;

that won't be necessary." He pursed his lips. "I think that covers it. If you have questions, ask them now, in an undertone near my ear. Have you?"

They shook their heads.

"Then we'll have lunch. The radio will be silent. We do not discuss business at the table. No one will speak but Mr. Goodwin and me."

He rose.

12

I wouldn't want to go through that twenty-eight hours
again.

Going through a forest where you know there are
snipers and one might be up any tree takes only guts
and sharp eyes. But if you don't *know* there are snipers
but only that there could be, that's different. Why all
the guts and the keen and careful eyes? We didn't
know the house was bugged, only that it might be. If
Jarvis or Kirby caught a finger in the bathroom door
and yelled ouch or goddammit, it might wreck the act,
but only *might,* and that was the hell of it. Every time
I made a trip upstairs to check that Saul or Fred or
Orrie was there in the hall, and that they hadn't got
fed up and started talking, I felt foolish. Grown men
don't look under the bed every night to see if there's a
burglar, though there *might* be one.

The two meals were screwy, with Wolfe and me, mostly Wolfe, carrying on with table talk, while the other five just ate and listened. Try it sometime. I couldn't even ask one of them to pass the butter; I could just point. And when we were doing something, for instance taking the boxes up to the potting room and stacking them, even I couldn't talk, because whom would I be talking to?

I left the house only once, late Wednesday afternoon, to call Hewitt from a booth and tell him the shipment had arrived in good condition, and to the garage to give Tom Halloran the picture.

There were bright spots, two of them on Wednesday and four on Thursday, when Jarvis observed Wolfe. Jarvis would stand at the foot of the stairs and study Wolfe coming down, at the top and study him going down, and in the hall and study him on the level. By the second session Thursday I knew Jarvis was pulling Wolfe's leg, enjoying the look on his face, but I was enjoying it too. Of course Kirby observed me the same way, but that was no hardship; on a normal day I go up and down those stairs a dozen times or more. What Kirby couldn't observe was my driving. They would probably be tailed all the way to Hewitt's, and if his style at the wheel was too different from mine it could make a smart G-man suspicious. Thursday morning I took him to the office and turned on the radio and discussed it for half an hour.

Looking back at it, I don't think we missed a single bet. Around eleven o'clock Wednesday night I went up to my room, which fronts on Thirty-fifth Street, paid no more attention to the curtains than usual, changed to pajamas, sat on the bed, and turned out the light on the bed stand. In a couple of minutes Fred and Orrie entered and undressed in the dark, and I got out and they got in. Saul slept on the sofa in the front room, and we didn't turn the lights on in there at all. We rarely do.

I mention a funny thing. As I turned the office lights out Wednesday night and got between sheets on the couch, I was thinking not of the trap we were setting and whether it was going to work, but of the couch in Sarah Dacos's apartment. What if the cleaning woman decided to turn the cushion over and looked under the spring? If I had stayed another five minutes maybe I could have found a better spot.

The two meals I mentioned were Wednesday's lunch and dinner. Thursday's breakfast and lunch were different because Fritz wasn't there. The arrangement was that Hewitt would have a car there for Fritz at eight o'clock, and it came right on time. I carried his bag out for him, and at the car door he shook my hand, looking glum. He was in no mood for producing masterpieces for a bunch of aristologists. Saul and I handled the breakfast problem, and for lunch we had cold cuts, including the sturgeon, which had been passed as edible, two bottles of champagne, and five kinds of cheese.

At 4:45 Thursday afternoon I was in the office with Saul and Fred and Orrie when Theodore Horstmann, the orchid nurse, who had been told to leave early, came downstairs, said good night, and left. Wolfe was up in his room. At 5:10 I went up to my room, turned on the lights, and started changing. I could have made sure that there was no chink in the curtains and just sat, but it wouldn't have been normal for me to bother about chinks and we damned well wanted everything normal. Wolfe, in his room, was doing likewise. At 5:40, dressed for dinner, I went back down to the office, and at 5:45 there was the sound of the elevator, and Wolfe appeared, also dressed. He and I started talking, no radio, about traffic problems. At 5:55 on the dot there was a faint sound of footsteps in the hall, and Jarvis and Kirby were there. Jarvis's dinner uniform was a big improvement on Wolfe's, which had seen better years, but Kirby's wasn't up to mine, which had set me back three Cs. They stood at the door. I told Wolfe I would wait in the car, went to the hall, held my coat for Kirby and handed him my hat, and stayed in the corner out of range as he opened the door, crossed the sill, and pulled the door shut. As Jarvis came and stood looking out through the one-way glass, with me at his elbow, the lights in the office went out, and I got Wolfe's coat and hat for Jarvis. In about half an hour which was really about six minutes the Heron showed and came to a stop at the curb. Jarvis flipped the light switch and the hall was dark, but I moved out of range until he was out and the door closed. I watched him and decided he was earning the extra grand. I had had no opinion about Kirby, since I don't know how I look when I walk, but I would have sworn it was Wolfe going down the steps, crossing the sidewalk, and getting into the car, if I hadn't known. The Heron rolled away, smooth, no jerks, like me, and I realized I had been holding my breath God knows how long.

The office was now empty if they had followed the script. Before the lights went out in the hall Wolfe had gone to the dark kitchen, Orrie to the dark dining room, and Saul and Fred through the connecting door

to the dark front room. I hadn't heard them, so no one
had. I put my hand in my side pocket to touch the
Marley .38, stepped to the door and touched the edge
to make sure it was closed, stood until my eyes were as
well adjusted to the dark as they would get, and sat
down on the chair at the wall opposite the rack.

I felt fine. The strain was over. It could have been
spoiled a hundred different ways, by either bad handling or bad luck, but here we were, all set, with nothing to do but wait. Either they had decided to do a bag
job or they hadn't, and that was their strain, not mine.
I didn't know what their score was on bag jobs, no
outsider does, but I knew of four in New York the past
year, definitely, and I had heard talk of several more.
It depended on whether Wragg believed that a G-man
had killed Althaus. If he did, ten to one they would
come. If he didn't, if he had somehow been satisfied
that his men were clean on the murder, they wouldn't
come. Whether the bait was good enough depended
on him, not on us. I felt fine.

When I decided half an hour had passed I went to
the door to look at my watch by the light coming
through the one-way glass, and when I saw 6:22 I felt
a little less fine. Wrong by eight minutes. I am supposed to be good at judging time, so evidently I wasn't
as unstrained as I thought I was. Instead of sitting, I
walked down the hall to the office door and felt still
less fine when I rubbed against the wall twice. That
was inexcusable. Of course going back to the front, toward the rectangle of light, was simple, but damn it,
I should be able to go straight down the center of the
hall I knew so well into the pitch dark. I did, three
times, and then went to the chair and sat.

I can't give the precise time that they came because I was determined not to look again until seven o'clock, but it was close to seven. Suddenly the dim light at the door was even dimmer and there they were. Two of them. A third was probably down on the sidewalk. One of them bent over to look at the lock, and the other stood at the top of the first step, his back to the door, facing the street.

Of course they had known the lock was a Rabson and had brought the right items, but no matter how good he was he wouldn't get a Rabson at the first stab, so there was no hurry. The door from the hall to the front room, open, was right there, four feet from the chair. I stepped to it, stuck my head in, let a low hiss through my teeth, and got one back. I walked to the dining room door, not touching the wall, did another hiss, and it was returned. Then I went and stood just outside the office door. They wouldn't flash a light the instant they made it in; they would stand and listen.

I have since argued with Saul about how long it took him. He says the door opened eight minutes after I hissed, and I say ten. Anyway it opened, and as it started I moved into the office, got my back against the wall to the left of the door, put my left hand behind me with a finger on the light switch, and took the Marley from my pocket with the right.

Once in, they didn't listen more than five seconds, which was bad technique. They came straight down the hall. With my head turned, I saw the faint gleam of a pencil flash grow brighter, then streak into the office, and then them. They came in three or four steps and stopped. The one with the flash started it around and in three seconds it would have hit me, so I sang out, "Play ball!" raised the Marley, and flipped the switch, and there was light.

One of them just gawked, but the one with the flash dropped it and started his hand inside his jacket. But not only did I have my gun out, Orrie was there beside me with his, and Saul's voice came from the door of the front room, "Strike one!" They turned their heads and saw two more guns.

"It looks bad," I said. "We don't even need to frisk you, you can't shoot in two directions at once. Mr. Wolfe!"

He was there. He must have left the kitchen when I called, "Play ball." I said, "Go around," but he had already started that way, to the right of the red leather chair, well out of their reach. At his desk he sat and eyed them—their profiles, since they were facing Orrie and me.

He spoke. "This is deplorable. Archie, call the police."

I moved. I didn't make as wide a detour as Wolfe had, but the program would go better without a scuffle, so I circled around. Halfway to my desk I stopped and said, "Look. If you jump me when I'm dialing you won't leave here on your feet. I suppose you know the law, crashers do. You're inside. If you try getting rough they'll plug you and all they'll get from the law is thanks."

"Balls." It was the big handsome one with a square jaw and square shoulders. The other one was taller, but skinny, with a face that showed the bones. Handsome was giving me the stony stare. "We're not crashers, and you know it."

"Like hell I do. You crashed. You can explain it to

the cops. I've warned you. Stay put. Start moving and you'll get stopped. One of them has a quick finger."

To get to the phone at my desk I had to give them my back. I did, and as I reached for the phone he snapped, "Cut the comedy, Goodwin. You know damn well what we are." He turned to Wolfe. "We're agents of the Federal Bureau of Investigation, and you know it. We have touched nothing, and we didn't intend to. We wanted to see you. When we rang there was no answer, and the door wasn't locked, and we came in."

"You lie," Wolfe said, just stating a fact. "Five men will swear that the door was locked and you didn't ring. Four of them heard you picking it. When you are searched, by the police, your tools will be found. Federal Bureau of Investigation? Pfui. Get the police, Archie, and tell them to send men capable of handling a pair of ruffians."

Before I turned to dial I said, "Fred," and bent a finger at him, and he came. Passing them, he barely gave them elbow room. He had once had an arm twisted by a G-man, and he would have welcomed a chance to even up. With the backs of his thighs against Wolfe's desk, facing them, his gun at his hip, he looked much nastier than he actually is. He is really a nice guy, with a wife and four children. As I started dialing I would have given a hundred to one that I wouldn't finish, and I didn't. At the fourth whirl Handsome blurted, "Hold it, Goodwin," and I stopped my finger and turned. He was slipping his left hand inside his coat. I cradled the phone and moved beside Fred. The G-man's hand came out with his little black leather fold. "Credentials," he said, and opened it and displayed it.

That was the ticklish spot. They're supposed to show it but hang on to it. Wolfe growled, "I'll inspect it," and Handsome made a move forward, and Fred's big left hand shot out and shoved him back. I put a hand out, palm up, but said nothing. He hesitated, not long, and put it on my palm. I said, "You too," to Skinny and stretched my arm. He had his fold already out and put it on top of the other one, and I turned and handed them to Wolfe. He looked at one and then the other, opened a drawer and got his big glass, inspected them through the glass, taking his time, returned the glass to the drawer, dropped the folds in on top of it, shut the drawer, and regarded them.

"Probably forged," he said. "The police laboratory can tell."

It must have taken a lot of control for them to hold tight. I would have admired them if my mind hadn't been occupied. They both went stiff but they didn't move; then Skinny said, "You fat sonofabitch."

Wolfe nodded. "A natural reaction. Let's make an assumption. Let us assume, merely for discussion, that you are in fact agents of the Federal Bureau of Investigation. Then you have a valid complaint, but not against me; against your colleagues who were gulled into thinking that this house was empty. You have nothing to apologize for."

He cleared his throat. "Now. Still on the assumption. I am going to keep your credentials as hostages. You can recover them, or your bureau can, only by an action at law which would disclose publicly how they got here, and I would of course have a counter action, since you entered my house illegally and were caught *flagrante delicto,* and I have four witnesses. I doubt if

your superiors would want to pay the price. So the
initiative is mine. You may go. All I wanted, still on the
assumption, was incontestable evidence that members
of the Federal Bureau of Investigation have committed
a felony and can be prosecuted, and I have it here in
my drawer. By the way, I haven't mentioned the gloves
you're wearing. Of course we have all noticed them.
That will be a corroborative detail if and when this
gets to a courtroom. You may go, gentlemen."

"Goddamn you." Handsome. "It will be a federal
courtroom. Those credentials are the property of federal officers."

"They may be. Even if they are I have a defense.
Abandoning the assumption, I find it difficult to believe
that federal officers of the law would enter my house
illegally, and obviously I am justified in keeping the
credentials until and unless their genuineness is established."

"How are you going to establish it?"

"I'll see. I shall await events. If they're genuine I
might be paid a call by one of your superiors—even
Mr. Wragg."

"You fat sonofabitch," Skinny said. He seemed limited
when under stress.

"Actually," Wolfe said, "I am being lenient. You
forced entry into my house, and for all I know you are
impersonating officers of the law. Two felonies. If you
are armed we should take your weapons and also
the tools you brought to open my door—and, no doubt,
to open doors and drawers in this office. And the gloves
you're wearing. I advise you to leave without delay.
These four men are not fond either of burglars or of

the FBI, and they would enjoy humiliating you. Confound it, go!"

They stood and looked at him. Handsome's line of vision was between Fred's shoulder and mine, and Skinny's was to the right of Fred. They exchanged glances, looked at Wolfe again, and moved. As they approached the door Orrie backed into the hall, his gun on them. He likes to point a gun. Saul went through the front room to the hall and turned the light on. Fred and I followed the G-men. When they neared the front door Saul opened it, and Orrie and Fred and I joined him to watch them descend to the sidewalk. Almost certainly there had been a third one, but he was nowhere in sight. They turned left, toward Tenth Avenue, but we didn't go out to see them to their car. Before we closed the door we examined the lock and found it intact. As I slid the bolt in Fred said that they must have the finest key collection in the world.

When we filed back into the office Wolfe was standing in the center of the rug, inspecting an object in his hand—the pencil flash Handsome had dropped. He tossed it onto my desk and roared, "Talk! All of you! Talk!"

Everybody laughed.

"I'm offering a reward," I said, loud. "A framed photograph of J. Edgar Hoover to anyone who will prove that it *is* bugged and they have a tape of that to send him."

"By God," Fred said, "if only they had tried something."

"I want champagne," Saul said.

"Make mine bourbon," Orrie said. "I'm hungry."

It was twenty minutes to eight. We went to the

kitchen, including Wolfe, everybody talking at once. Wolfe began getting things from the refrigerator— caviar, *pâté de foie gras,* sturgeon, a whole smoked pheasant. Saul opened the freezer to get ice for champagne. Orrie and I got bottles from the cupboard. Fred asked if he could use the phone to call his wife, and I said yes and give her my love, but Wolfe spoke.

"Tell her you will stay here tonight. You will all stay. In the morning Archie will take those things to the bank, and you'll go with him. They will probably do nothing, but they might try anything. Fred, tell nothing of this to your wife, or to anyone else. It isn't finished, it's only well started. If you men want something hot I can have Yorkshire Buck in twenty minutes if Archie will poach the eggs."

They all said no, which suited me fine. I hate to poach eggs.

An hour later we were having a pleasant evening. The three guests and I were in the front room, in a tight game of pinochle, and Wolfe was in his one and only chair in the office, reading a book. The book was *The FBI Nobody Knows.* He was either gloating or doing research, I didn't know which.

At ten o'clock I had to excuse myself from the card table briefly; Wolfe had said he wanted to call Hewitt then, when the aristologists would presumably have finished their meal. I went to the office and made the call. Wolfe told Hewitt it had worked perfectly and thanked him. Hewitt said they had found the stand-ins very entertaining; Jarvis had recited passages from Shakespeare and Kirby had mimicked President Johnson and Barry Goldwater and Alfred Lunt. Wolfe said to give them his regards, and I went back to pinochle and Wolfe to his book.

But there was another interruption a little after eleven o'clock. The phone rang, and Wolfe hates to answer it, so I went and got it at my desk.

"Nero Wolfe's residence, Archie Goodwin speaking."

"This is Richard Wragg, Goodwin." The voice was a drawl, smooth and low-pitched. "I want to speak to Wolfe."

We had known that might happen, and I had instructions.

"I'm afraid you can't, Wragg. He's engaged."

"I want to see him."

"Good idea. He thought you might. Say here, his office, at eleven in the morning?"

"I want to see him tonight. Now."

"I'm sorry, Wragg, that isn't possible. He's very busy. The earliest would be eleven in the morning."

"What's he busy at?"

"He's reading a book. *The FBI Nobody Knows.* In half an hour he'll be in bed."

"I'll be there at eleven."

It sounded as if he cradled it with a bang, but I could have imagined that. I turned to Wolfe. "I called him Wragg because that's his name. Eleven o'clock tomorrow morning. As expected."

"And desired. We must confer. When your game is finished."

I rose. "It won't take long. I just melded three hundred and forty."

13

I need, and nearly always get, a good eight hours'
sleep, but that night I got six. At 1:10, with Wolfe gone
up to bed, and also Fred and Orrie, and Saul on the
sofa in the front room, I was about to crawl in on the
couch when the doorbell rang. It was Fritz and Jarvis
and Kirby, and when I saw Kirby stagger across the
threshold I wondered what ditch the Heron was in. I
asked him where the car was and he just goggled at
me, his lips pressed tight. Thinking he was sticking to
the instructions, I told him he could talk now, and Fritz
said he could not talk now because he was too drunk,
and added that the car was out in front, perfectly all
right, but only the good God knew how it had got
there. He took them up to their room in the elevator,
and I put on shoes and my overcoat over pajamas, and
went out and took the Heron to the garage. Not a
scratch.

The first number on the program for Friday was scheduled for 8:30. At 7:45 I turned on the will power and rolled out, got my arms full of blankets and sheets and pillow, and made it up to my room. When I came out of the bathroom after showering and shaving, Fred and Orrie were sitting on the edge of the bed, yawning. I remarked that we would be leaving in an hour and twenty minutes and they told me to go soak my head, but I already had. I was expecting to have to manage my own breakfast, but as I was going downstairs Fritz emerged from Wolfe's room, having delivered the breakfast tray nearly on time. It was 8:28, and I went to the office and started the day by dialing Mrs. Bruner's number and got her. I told her I was sorry to disturb her so early in the day, but I had an important message, and would she please go out to a booth and ring me at a certain number, which I gave her, at 9:45 or as soon after as possible. She said it would interfere with an appointment and how important was it, and I said extremely, and she said all right.

So we could take our time at breakfast, and it was just as well. Fritz knows that Saul and Fred and Orrie all like eggs *au beurre noir*, so that was the main item, with toast and bacon, and two rounds for each of us, two eggs to a round, added up to sixteen eggs. The expense account for that operation was going to be a lulu.

With the credentials in my pocket, I left the house with my bodyguard at 9:40, walked to the drugstore at the corner, and stationed myself near the booth. With my understanding of women, I was prepared to wait up to twenty minutes, but at 9:46 it rang, just as a man who had entered was heading for the booth. As I

lifted the receiver I decided that he was not a G-man
come to take the call; he didn't look the part.

Mrs. Bruner said she hoped it was really important
because she would be late for her appointment.

"You couldn't possibly have any appointment half as
important," I told her. "Forget appointments. You are
to be at Mr. Wolfe's office at a quarter to eleven, not
one second later."

"This morning? I can't."

"You can and must. You have told me twice that you
didn't like my tone, but that was nothing compared
to the tone you'll hear unless you say you'll be there.
Mr. Wolfe might even return the hundred grand."

"But why? What is it?"

"I'm just the messenger boy. You'll find out when you
come. It's not just important, it's vital."

Short silence. "A quarter to eleven?"

"Or earlier."

More silence. "Very well. I'll be there."

"Wonderful. You're the perfect client. If you weren't
rich I'd marry you."

"What did you say?"

"Nothing." I hung up.

I didn't feel vital, with only six hours' sleep, but I
felt important as I walked crosstown to the Conti-
nental Bank and Trust Company on Lexington Avenue
with the winter wind at my back. Not many men have
had such a bodyguard—the best operative between the
two oceans plus two damned good ones. If you think
we were overdoing it, what if I stumbled and cracked
my skull, or what if I ran into a siren who dazzled me
and she turned out to be a G-woman? Anyway, they
were there in the house and a walk would do them

good. At the bank I went downstairs first, to the safe-
deposit box, and stashed the credentials. Upstairs, as
I cashed a check for five grand to replenish the cash
reserve in the safe, I was thinking that it had been
just nine days, to the hour, since I had been there to
deposit the retainer. I had thought then that there was
one chance in a million. Now . . .

We had to step on it to get back to the old brownstone by a quarter to eleven, and we barely made it.
We were in the hall, shedding coats, when I saw Mrs.
Bruner's Rolls pull up out in front. When she reached
the stoop I had the door open. Fred and Orrie started
off, but I called them back:

"Mrs. Bruner," I said, "how would you like to meet
three men who, working for you, rode sixty miles in a
truck, curled up inside wooden boxes with the lids
screwed on? And who stood for twenty minutes last
evening with guns pointed at two FBI men while Mr.
Wolfe told them things?"

"Why—I would like to."

"I thought so. Mr. Saul Panzer. Mr. Fred Durkin. Mr.
Orrie Cather. You will spend some time with Mr. Panzer. If you don't mind, I'll put your coat in the front
room. Richard Wragg, the top G-man in New York, is
coming, and shouldn't see it."

Her eyes were wide but her mouth was closed. I
decided to marry her in spite of her pile. As I took her
coat Fred and Orrie headed for the stairs, to hang
around outside the South Room and not let Jarvis and
Kirby come down and interrupt the conversation.

At the kitchen end of the hall there is an alcove on
the left, and around the corner in the alcove there is a
hole in the wall at eye level. On the alcove side of the

hole there is a sliding panel, and on the office side the hole is covered by a trick picture of a waterfall. If you stand in the alcove and open the panel you have a view of most of the office through the waterfall, and of course you can hear.

Taking Mrs. Bruner to the alcove, followed by Saul, I slid the panel and showed her the hole. "As I said," I told her, "Wragg is coming and will be in the office with Mr. Wolfe and me. Mr. Panzer will bring the stool from the kitchen, and you'll sit here on it, and he'll stand here. It will last anywhere from ten minutes to two hours, I don't know. You won't understand everything you hear, but you'll understand enough. If you feel a cough or sneeze coming, go to the kitchen fast on your toes. Saul will motion to you if—"

The doorbell rang. I stuck my head around the alcove corner, and there he was on the stoop, five minutes ahead of time. I told Saul to get the stool, and as he headed for the kitchen I started down the hall. At the door I looked back, got a nod from him at the alcove corner, and opened the door.

Richard Wragg was forty-four years old. He lived in an apartment in Brooklyn with a wife and two children and had been with the FBI fifteen years. Detectives know things. He was about my height, with a long face and a pointed chin, and would be bald on top in four years, or maybe three. He didn't offer to shake, but he turned his back as I peeled his coat off, so he trusted me to a certain extent. When I ushered him to the office and to the red leather chair he stood and looked the room over, and I thought he was too interested in the picture of the waterfall, but perhaps not. He was still standing when the sound of the elevator came and Wolfe entered and stopped short of his desk to say, "Mr. Wragg? I'm Nero Wolfe. Be seated." As he went to his chair Wragg sat down, found he was only on the edge, and slid back.

Their eyes met. From my angle I couldn't see Wolfe's, but Wragg's were straight and steady.

"I know about you," Wragg said, "but I've never met you."

Wolfe nodded. "Some paths don't cross."

"But now ours have. I assume that this is being recorded."

"No. There is equipment, but it isn't turned on. We might as well ignore such matters. I have assumed for a week that everything said in this house was overheard. You may have a device on your person. I might have my recorder going—though, as I say, I haven't. Let's ignore it."

"We haven't bugged this house."

Wolfe's shoulders went up an eighth of an inch and down. "Ignore it. You wanted to see me?"

Wragg's fingers were curled over the ends of the chair arms. At ease. "As you expected. We don't need to waste time shadow-boxing. I want the credentials you took from two of my men last night by force."

Wolfe turned a hand over. Also at ease. "But you *are* shadow-boxing. Retract that 'by force.' The force was initiated by them. They entered my house by force. I merely met force with force."

"I want those credentials."

"Do you retract your 'by force'?"

"No. I acknowledge that your retort was valid. Give me the credentials and we'll talk on even terms."

"Pfui. Are you a dunce, or do you take me for one?

I have no intention of talking on even terms. You came
to see me because I constrained you to, but if you came
to talk nonsense you may as well leave. Shall I describe
the situation as I see it?"

"Yes."

Wolfe turned his head. "Archie. Mrs. Bruner's letter
engaging me."

I went to the safe and got it. As I returned Wolfe
nodded at Wragg, and I handed it to him. I stood
there, and when he had read it I put out a hand. He
read it again, slower, and handed it over without looking up at me, and I went to my desk and put it in a
drawer.

"Quite a document," he told Wolfe. "For the record,
if there was any espionage of Mrs. Bruner or her
family or associates, which I am not admitting, it was
in connection with a security check."

Wolfe nodded. "You say that, of course. A routine
lie. I am describing the situation. Your men departed
last night, leaving their credentials in my possession,
because they dared not call on the police to rescue
them. They knew that if a citizen charged them with
the crime of entering his house illegally, and pushed
the charge, the sympathy of the New York police and
the District Attorney would be with the citizen. You
know it too. You will not take legal steps to recover
the credentials, so they will not be recovered. I shall
keep them. I suggest an exchange. You engage to stop
all surveillance of Mrs. Bruner and her family and
associates, including the tap on her telephone, and I—"

"I haven't conceded the surveillance."

"Bah. If you— No. It's simpler to rephrase it. Disre-
garding the past, you engage that from six o'clock to-

day there will be by your bureau no surveillance of
Mrs. Bruner or her family or associates, or her house,
which includes a wiretap, and no surveillance of Mr.
Goodwin or me, or my house. I engage to leave the
credentials where they are, in my safe-deposit box, to
take no action against your men for their invasion of
my premises, and to make public no disclosure of it.
That's the situation, and that's my offer."

"Do you mean engage in writing?"

"Not unless you prefer it."

"I don't. Nothing in writing. I'll agree to the surveillance part, but I must have the credentials."

"You won't get them." Wolfe pointed a finger at him.
"Understand this, Mr. Wragg. I'll surrender the credentials only if ordered to by a court, and I'll contest
the order with all my resources and those of my client.
You may—"

"Damn it, you have four witnesses!"

"I know. But judges and juries are sometimes whim-
sical. They may capriciously doubt the credibility of
witnesses, even five of them—counting me. It would be
fatuous for you to question my good faith. I have no
desire to enter into a mortal feud with your bureau;
my sole purpose is to do the job I have been hired for.
As long as you harass or annoy neither my client nor
me, I shall have no use either for the credentials or
for my witnesses."

Wragg looked at me. I thought he was going to ask
me something, but no, I was just a place to give his
eyes a rest from Wolfe while he answered some question he had asked himself. It took him a while. Finally
he went back to Wolfe.

"You've left something out," he said. "You say your

sole purpose is to do the job you've been hired for. Then why have you been investigating a homicide we have no connection with? Why has Goodwin gone twice to see Mrs. David Althaus, and twice to Morris Althaus's apartment, and why did you have those six people here last Thursday evening?"

Wolfe nodded. "You think one of your men shot Morris Althaus."

"I do not. That's absurd."

Wolfe got testy. "Confound it, sir, can't you talk sense? What could they have conceivably been after when they invaded my house? You suspected that I had somehow discovered that three of your men had been in Morris Althaus's apartment the night he was killed, as indeed I had. They had reported to you that he was dead when they arrived, but you didn't believe them. At least you doubted them. I don't know why; you know them; I don't. And you suspected or feared that I had not only learned that they were there but had also secured evidence that they, one of them, had killed him. Talk sense."

"You still haven't told me why you were investigating a homicide."

"Isn't that obvious? Because I had learned that your men had been there."

"How did you learn that?"

Wolfe shook his head. "That's reserved."

"Have you been in touch with Inspector Cramer?"

"No. I haven't seen or spoken with him for months."

"Or the District Attorney's office?"

"No."

"Are you going to continue the investigation?"

A corner of Wolfe's mouth went up. "You know, Mr.

Wragg, I am both able and willing to relieve your mind, but first I must be assured that I have done my job. Have you accepted my offer? Do you assure me that from six o'clock this afternoon there will be no surveillance of any kind by your bureau of Mrs. Bruner or anyone connected with her?"

"Yes. That's settled."

"Satisfactory. Now I ask you to make another engagement. I want you to return here, when requested by me, and bring the bullet which one of your men picked up on the floor of Morris Althaus's apartment."

It probably wasn't easy to faze Richard Wragg. You don't get to be the top G-man at the most important spot, next to Washington, if you faze easy. But that got him. His mouth came open. It took him only two seconds to close it, but he had been fazed.

"Now *you're* not talking sense," he said.

"But I am. If you'll bring me that bullet when I ask for it, it is next to certain—I am tempted to say certain —that I can establish that Althaus was not killed by one of your men."

"God, you're raw." Wragg's mouth wasn't open now. His eyes were narrowed to slits. "If I had such a bullet I might bring it just to call you."

"Oh, you have it." Wolfe was patient. "What happened that night in Althaus's apartment? A person I'll call X—I could give a better name, for now X will do —shot him with his own gun. The bullet went through him to the wall and fell to the floor. X departed, taking the gun. Soon your three men arrived, entering just as they entered this house last night. Shall I go into detail?"

"Yes."

"Here they didn't ring the bell because it was known, so they thought, that the house was empty. It had been under surveillance for a week. They rang Althaus's bell, and probably his telephone, but he didn't answer because he was dead. After they had searched the apartment and got what they had come for, it occurred to them that you would suspect that one of them had killed him, and as evidence that they hadn't they took the bullet, which was there on the floor. That violated a law of the State of New York, but they had already violated one, why not another? They took it and gave it to you with their report."

He flipped a hand. "Possibly their bringing the bullet, instead of convincing you of their innocence, had the opposite effect, but I won't speculate about your mental processes, why you didn't believe them. As I said, you know your men. But of course you still have the bullet, and I'm going to want it."

Wragg's eyes had stayed narrow. "Listen, Wolfe. You trapped us once, damn you. You trapped us good. But not again. If I had that bullet I wouldn't be sap enough to give it to *you*."

"You will be a sap if you don't." Wolfe made a face. There are a few slang words he likes and uses, but "sap" isn't one of them, and he had uttered it. He straightened his face. "I concern myself with this because I have an obligation—to the person from whom I learned that your men were there that night—and I don't like obligations. Exposing the murderer will cancel that debt and, incidentally, relieve your mind. Wouldn't you like it to be established that Althaus was not killed by one of your men? Bring me that bullet, and it will be. I make another offer: bring me that bul-

let, and if your men are not cleared within a month
by disclosure of the murderer I'll give you those credentials. It shouldn't take a month, probably not even
a week."

Wragg's eyes were open. "You'll return the credentials?"

"Yes."

"You say 'disclosure.' Disclosed to whom?"

"To you. Disclosed sufficiently to convince you that
your men are innocent—of murder, that is."

"You make an offer. What guarantee would I have?"

"My word."

"How good is your word?"

"Better than yours. Much better, if that book is to be
believed. No man alive can say that I have ever dis-
honored my word."

Wragg ignored the dig. "When would you want the
bullet—if I had it?"

"I don't know. Possibly later today. Or tomorrow.
I would want to receive it from your hands."

"If I had it." Wragg stood up. "I have some thinking
to do. I'm promising nothing. I'll—"

"But you are. You have. No surveillance of my client
or me."

"That, yes. I mean—you know what I mean." He
moved, then stopped and turned. "You'll be here all
day?"

"Yes. But if you telephone, my line is tapped."

He didn't think that was funny. I doubt if he would
have thought anything whatever was funny. As I followed him to the hall and held his coat and handed
him his hat, he didn't even know I was there. When I
turned from shutting the door behind him I saw the

client entering the office, Saul at her heels, and I decided not to marry her. She should have waited for me to come and escort her. When I reached the office there was a tableau. Mrs. Bruner and Saul were standing side by side at Wolfe's desk, looking down at him, and he was leaning back with his eyes closed. It was a nice picture, and I stopped at the door to enjoy it. Half a minute. A full minute. That was enough, since she had appointments, and as I crossed to them I asked, "Could you hear all right?"

Wolfe's eyes opened. Not answering me, she told him, "You're an incredible man. Utterly incredible. I didn't really think you could do it. Incredible. Is there *anything* you couldn't do?"

He straightened up. "Yes, madam," he said, "there is. I couldn't put sense in a fool's brain. I have tried. I could mention others. You understand why it was desirable for you to come. The letter you signed says 'if you get the result I desire.' Are you satisfied?"

"Of course I am. Incredible."

"I find it a little hard to believe, myself. Please sit down. There is something I must tell you."

"There certainly is." She went to the red leather chair. Saul went to a yellow one and I to mine. She asked, "What was the trap you set?"

Wolfe shook his head. "Not that. That can wait. Mr. Goodwin will give you all the details at your and his convenience. I must tell you not what has been done but what should now be done. You are my client and I must protect you from embarrassment. How discreet are you?"

She frowned. "Why do you ask that?"

"Please answer it. How discreet are you? Can you be trusted with a secret?"

"Yes."

His head turned. "Archie?"

Damn him anyway. It was all right to embarrass *me*. What if I changed my mind again and decided to marry her?

"Yes," I said, "if I know where you're headed, and I think I do."

"Of course you do." To her: "I wish to save you the embarrassment of having your secretary taken from your office by the police, perhaps in your presence, to be questioned regarding a murder which she probably committed."

He had only fazed Wragg, but that staggered the client. Her mouth didn't drop open; she just stared, speechless.

"I say probably," Wolfe said, "but it is barely short of certainty. The victim was Morris Althaus. Mr. Goodwin will give you the details of this too, but not now, not until the situation has been resolved. I would have preferred not to give you even the bare fact now, but as my client you merit my protection. I wish to make a suggestion."

"I don't believe it," she said. "I want the details *now*."

"You won't get them." He was curt. "I have had a trying week, and night, and day. If you make this difficult too I'll leave the room and you'll leave the house, and probably question Miss Dacos. That will alarm her and she'll skedaddle, and after the police find her and bring her back they will have questions for you—civil questions, but many of them. Do you want that?"

"No."

"Do you think I would make so grave an accusation idly?"

"No."

"Then I have a suggestion." He looked at the wall clock. Five minutes past noon. "What time does Miss Dacos go to lunch?"

"It varies. She eats there, in the breakfast room, usually around one o'clock."

"Then Mr. Panzer will go with you now. Tell her you are going to have the office redecorated—painted, plastered, whatever suits—and you won't need her the remainder of this week. Mr. Panzer will start the preparations immediately. She, your secretary, is going to be taken, but at least she won't be taken from your house. I do not want a murderer taken into custody in the house of my client. Do you?"

"No."

"Nor would you have wanted the disagreeable surprise of sitting in your office with your secretary and having the police suddenly appear and drag her out."

"No."

"Then you may thank me at your convenience for preventing it. You're not in a humor to thank anyone for anything at the moment. Shall Mr. Panzer go in your car with you, or separately? You could discuss it with him on the way. He is *not* a fool."

She looked at me and back at Wolfe. "Can Mr. Goodwin go?"

Saul has not yet heard the last of that. It didn't change my decision about marriage because I prefer to do the courting myself, but it gave me one on Saul. Wolfe told her no, Mr. Goodwin had work to do, and the poor woman had to settle for Saul. He brought her coat from the front room and held it for her, and I admit I had a pang. By the time they got to Seventy-fourth Street she would be appreciating him. Not wanting to intrude, I didn't go to the hall with them.

When the sound came of the front door closing Wolfe cocked his head at me and demanded, "Say something."

"Bejabers," I said. "Will that do? A guy I know named Birnbaum uses it to show he's not prejudiced. Bejabers."

"Satisfactory."

"All of that."

"Our telephone is still tapped. Will you see Mr. Cramer before lunch?"

"After would be better. He'll be in a better humor. It will take them only an hour or so to get the warrant."

"Very well. But don't— Yes, Fred?"

Fred Durkin, at the door, announced, "They want breakfast."

14

The office of the inspector in command of Homicide South on West Twentieth Street is not really shabby, but it's not for show. The linoleum floor has signs of wear, Cramer's desk would appreciate a sanding job, I have never seen the windows really clean, and the chairs, all but Cramer's, are plain, honest, hard wood. As I put my fundament on one of them at 2:35 p.m. he snapped at me, "I told you don't come and don't phone."

I nodded. "But it's okay now and I had to. Mr. Wolfe—"

"What's okay?"

"He has earned the hundred grand *and* a fee."

"The hell he has. He has got them to quit on that Mrs. Bruner?"

"Yes. Bejabers. But we haven't filled your order. We have—"

"I didn't give any order."

"Oh, all right. We have learned that it wasn't a G-man who shot Morris Althaus. We think we know who did, and we think we know how it can be tagged. I'm not going to tell you how we put the screws on the FBI. That's not what I came for, and Mr. Wolfe will enjoy telling you some time at your leisure, and you'll enjoy listening. It was the longest shot he has ever played, and it hit. I'm here to talk homicide."

"Go ahead. Talk."

I reached to my breast pocket, took something out, and handed it to him. "I doubt if you've seen that before," I said, "but one or more of your men have. It was in a drawer in Althaus's bedroom. His mother gave me the keys, so don't book me for illegal entry. Look at the back."

He turned it over and read the poetry.

"That," I said, "is a take-off of the last four lines of the second stanza of Keats's 'Ode on a Grecian Urn.' Rather clever. It was written by Miss Sarah Dacos, Mrs. Bruner's secretary, who lives at Sixty-three Arbor Street, second floor, below Althaus's apartment. The way I know, I got samples of her handwriting from Mrs. Bruner. Here they are." I got them from a pocket and handed them over. "By the way, she saw the three G-men leave the house. From her window. Remember that when you're working on her."

"Working on her for what? This?" He tapped the photograph.

"No. The main thing I came for was to place a bet. One will get you fifty that if you get a warrant and comb her apartment you'll get something you'll appreciate. The sooner the better." I stood up. "That's all for now. We would—"

"Like hell it's all." His red round face was redder. "Sit down. I'll work on *you*. What will we find and when did you put it there?"

"I didn't. Listen. As you know, when you deal with me you're dealing with Mr. Wolfe. You also know that I always stick to instructions. For the present I'm through. I stand mute. Any time you spend barking at me will be wasted. Get the warrant and use it, and if you find anything Mr. Wolfe will be glad to discuss it."

"I'll discuss it with you first. You'll stay right here."

"Not unless I'm put under arrest." I got sore. "What more do you want, for God's sake? You've had this homicide nearly two months! We've had it one week!"

I turned and walked out. It was even money I would be stopped, if not there by him then down on the ground floor when I left the elevator. But all I got, from the bull on duty in the downstairs hall, who knew me by sight, was a nod, not too friendly but almost human. I didn't loiter.

I crossed town to Sixth Avenue and turned south. Everything was under control at the old brownstone. Ashley Jarvis and Dale Kirby, not too badly hung over, had been fed a hearty breakfast and handed the bonus of one grand each, and had departed. Fred and Orrie had each been given three Cs for two days' work, not to mention nights, miles above scale, and had also departed. Saul was up at Mrs. Bruner's office getting ready to paint or plaster, whichever suited. Wolfe would of course be reading a book, certainly not *The FBI Nobody Knows*, since he knew them now, anyhow three of them, and at four o'clock he would go up to

the plant rooms, back on schedule. Since I never take
an afternoon nap, even when I'm short on sleep, I could
go for a walk, and did.

I came to a stop across the street from 63 Arbor
Street. But the thermometer outside the front-room
window had said sixteen above zero when I got up,
and it had climbed only about five notches since,
and I had the keys in my pocket, so I crossed the street,
entered, and mounted the two flights to Althaus's
apartment. I include this in the report not because it
changed anything, but because I remember so well my
state of mind. Fifty-three hours had passed since I had
put the gun under the box spring, and that was time
enough for a healthy girl to find a dozen guns and put
them somewhere else. If it wasn't there we would now
be out on a limb, and a shaky one, since I had told
Cramer. He knew Wolfe hadn't sent me there just on
a suspicion or a hunch; he knew we knew there was
something hot in that apartment, and if it was gone we
were in for it. If I told him about the gun I would be
admitting I had tampered with evidence; if I didn't, I
would be suspected of something even worse, and
good-by licenses.

You may not be interested in my state of mind, but
believe me I was. At one of the front windows in
Althaus's living room I pushed the drape aside and
pressed my forehead against the glass so I could see
the sidewalk below. That was fairly dumb, but a state
of mind can make you dumb. It was 3:25. I had left
Cramer only thirty-five minutes ago, and it would take
them about an hour to get the warrant, so what was I
expecting to see? Also the glass was cold, and I backed
away a couple of inches. But I was really on edge, and

now and then I put my forehead to the glass again, and
after a while I did see something. Sarah Dacos came
in view on the sidewalk with a big brown paper bag
under her arm and turned in at the entrance. It was
ten minutes to four. Seeing her didn't help my state of
mind any. I had nothing against Sarah Dacos. Of
course I had nothing for her either. A woman who
sends a bullet through a man's pump may or may not
deserve some sympathy, but she damn well can't expect a stranger to take a detour if she gets in his way
while he's doing a job.

Bending my ears, I heard the door of her apartment
open and close.

At a quarter past four two police cars stopped out
in front. One of them found a spot at the curb and the
other one double-parked, and I recognized all three of
the homicide dicks who got out and headed for Number 63. One of them, Sergeant Purley Stebbins, was
probably thinking of me as he pushed the button at
the door. He hates to find Nero Wolfe or me in the
same county with a homicide, and here he was on an
errand we were responsible for. I wanted to go to the
hall to hear the conversation when he showed her the
warrant, but didn't. He might smell me and it would
hold up the search.

It took them not more than ten minutes to find it.
They entered the apartment at 4:21, that was when I
heard the door close, and Purley left the house with
her at 4:43. I'm allowing twelve minutes for him to ask
her a few questions after he got the gun. I stood at the
window and watched Purley get in the car with her,
and the car pull off, and then went and sat on the
couch. Since he had taken her, the question about the

gun was answered. I stayed on the couch a few minutes while my state of mind got adjusted.

I got my hat and coat and went. There was still a NYPD car out in front, waiting for the two dicks still in the apartment, and the driver might know me, but so what? I hadn't recognized him from the window, and I don't know if he knew me or not. As I walked past the car, no hurry, he gave me a hard eye, but that could have been because I had come out of that house.

I walked home. It was a little after half past five, dark, when I mounted the stoop and let myself in. I went to the kitchen, got a glass of milk, and asked Fritz, "Has he told you that we're off the hook?"

"No." He was inspecting carrots.

"Well, we are. Say anything you want to on the phone. Resume with your girl friends. If a stranger speaks to you, do as you please. Do you want some good advice?"

"Yes."

"Hit him for a raise. I am. By the way, I haven't asked you about the dinner last night. Did you feed them good?"

He leveled his eyes at me. "Archie, that is never to be mentioned. That terrible day. *Epouvantable.* My mind was here with you. I don't know what I did, I don't know what was served. I will forget it if possible."

"Hewitt said on the phone that they stood and applauded you."

"But certainly. They were polite. I *know* I put no truffles in the *Périgourdine.*"

"Good God. I'm glad I wasn't there. Okay, we'll forget it. May I have a carrot? It's wonderful with milk."

He said certainly, and I helped myself.

I was at my desk, making out checks to pay bills, when Wolfe came down from the plant rooms. Though he hadn't said so I knew he was as much on edge as I had been, and as he went to his desk I turned my head and said, "Relax. They got the gun."

"How do you know?"

I told him, beginning with the conversation with Cramer and ending with the conversation with Fritz. He asked if I had got a receipt for the photograph.

"No," I said, "he wasn't in a mood for signing receipts. I had told him that Althaus hadn't been killed by a G-man, and that hurt."

"No doubt. Will Mr. Wragg be at his office?"

"He could be."

"Get him."

I turned and got the phone, but as I started to dial the doorbell rang. I cradled it and went to the hall for a look, turned, and said, "You can ask him for the receipt."

He took a breath. "Is he alone?"

I told him yes and went to the front and opened the door. Cramer didn't have a carton of milk for me. He had nothing at all for me, not even a nod. When I had his coat he made for the office, and when I got there he was planted in the red leather chair and talking. I got the end of it: ". . . and I might have known better. God knows I *should* know better." He switched to me as I sat. "Where did you get that gun and when did you put it there?"

"Confound it," Wolfe growled, "you shouldn't have come. You should have waited until you had arranged your mind. Archie, get Mr. Wragg."

When Cramer is boiling it isn't easy to stop the

steam, but that did, the name Wragg. I didn't see him clamp his jaw and glare at Wolfe, I only knew he did, because my back was turned as I dialed LE 5-7700. I was supposing it would take patience and staying power to get through to the top, but not at all. Apparently word had been passed down that a call from Nero Wolfe had priority, which was a good sign. In no time the smooth low-pitched drawl was in my ear, and in Wolfe's too, for he had picked up his phone. I stayed on.

"Wolfe?"

"Yes. Mr. Wragg?"

"Yes."

"I'm ready for that bullet. Now. As we agreed. Bring the bullet, and I surrender the credentials if you are not satisfied within a month. I think it will be sooner, much sooner."

No hesitation. "I'll come."

"Now?"

"Yes."

As we hung up Wolfe asked me, "How long will it take him?" I said twenty minutes or less, that he wouldn't have to scout for a taxi, and Wolfe turned to Cramer. "Mr. Wragg will be here in twenty minutes. I suggest—"

"Wragg of the FBI?"

"Yes. I suggest that you postpone your onslaught until he arrives—and, perhaps, goes—and meanwhile I'll describe an operation which has been concluded. I have told Mr. Wragg that I will make no public disclosure of it, but you are not the public, and since you made it possible I owe it to you. But it will help in dealing with him if you will answer two questions. Was a gun found in Miss Dacos's apartment?"

"Certainly. I just asked Goodwin when he put it there, and I'm going to ask him again."

"You may not after we finish with Mr. Wragg. Was it the gun Morris Althaus had a permit for?"

"Yes."

"That will simplify matters greatly. Now that operation . . ."

He described it, and he reports almost as well as I do—better, if you like long words. There was no point in leaving Hewitt's name out since the FBI knew all about it, and he gave all the details. When he came to the scene in the office, with the two G-men completely surrounded by guns and him dropping their credentials in his drawer, I saw something I had never seen before and will probably never see again, a broad smile on the face of Inspector Cramer. And it was there again when, reporting the conversation with Wragg that morning, Wolfe came to where he had told him that his word was much better. I was thinking that he might even pop up to go to Wolfe and pat him on the back when the doorbell rang and I went to answer it.

I have mentioned that Wragg was fazed when Wolfe asked him to bring the bullet, but that was nothing compared to the jolt he got when he walked into the office and saw Cramer. I was behind him and couldn't see his face, but I saw him go stiff and his fingers curl. Cramer, on his feet, started a hand out but took it back.

As I brought a yellow chair Wragg spoke to Wolfe. "Your word? Better than mine? You goddam skunk!"

"Sit down," Wolfe said. "Whether my word is better

or not, my brain is. I don't judge a situation before I understand it. Mr. Cramer is—"

"All agreements are off."

"Pfui. You're not a donkey. Mr. Cramer is regretting that he surmised that a member of your bureau was a murderer. If you sit down and compose yourself he may tell you so."

"I have no apologies for anybody," Cramer growled. He turned his head to make sure the red leather chair was still there, and sat. "Anyone who withholds information—"

"No," Wolfe snapped. "If you gentlemen must contend, that's your affair, but not in my office. I want to resolve a situation, not tangle it. I like eyes at a level, Mr. Wragg. Be seated."

"Resolve it how?"

"Sit down and I'll tell you."

He didn't want to. He looked at Cramer, he even looked at me, like a general surveying a battlefield and watching his flanks. He didn't like it, but he sat.

Wolfe turned a palm up. "Actually," he said, "the situation isn't tangled at all. We all want the same thing. I want to get rid of an obligation. You, Mr. Wragg, want it made manifest that your men are not criminally implicated in a murder. You, Mr. Cramer, want to identify and bring to account the person who killed Morris Althaus. It couldn't be simpler. You, Mr. Wragg, give Mr. Cramer the bullet you have in your pocket and tell him where it came from. You, Mr. Cramer, have a comparison made of that bullet with one fired from the gun which was taken this afternoon from the apartment of Sarah Dacos, and along with other evidence which no doubt your men are securing now, that will settle it. There is no—"

"I haven't said I have a bullet in my pocket."

"Nonsense. I advise you to pull in your horns, Mr. Wragg. Mr. Cramer has good reason to suppose that you have on your person an essential item of evidence in a homicide which occurred in his jurisdiction. Under the statutes of the State of New York he may legally search you, here and now, and get it. Is that correct, Mr. Cramer?"

"Yes."

"But," Wolfe told Wragg, "that shouldn't be necessary. You do have a brain. Obviously it is to your interest and that of your bureau that you give Mr. Cramer that bullet."

"The hell it is," Wragg said. "And one of my men gets on the stand and says under oath that he was in that apartment and took it? The hell it is."

Wolfe shook his head. "No. No indeed. You wouldn't. You give Mr. Cramer your word, here privately, that that's where the bullet came from, and one of *his* men gets on the stand and says under oath that he took it from that apartment. There will—"

"My men are not perjurers," Cramer said.

"Bah. This is not being recorded. If Mr. Wragg hands you a bullet and says it was found on the floor of Morris Althaus's apartment around eleven o'clock in the evening of Friday, November twentieth, will you believe him?"

"Yes."

"Then save your posing for audiences that will appreciate it. This one isn't sufficiently naïve. I don't think—"

"He might not be posing," Wragg cut in. "He might go on the stand himself and tell how he got it. Then I'm called to the stand."

Wolfe nodded. "True. He might. But he wouldn't. If he did, I too would be called to the stand, and Mr. Goodwin, and a much larger audience than this one would learn how the murderer of Morris Althaus had been disclosed after the police and the District Attorney had spent eight futile weeks on it. He wouldn't."

"Damn you," Cramer said. "Both of you."

Wolfe looked at the clock. "It's past my dinner hour, gentlemen. I've said all I have to say, and I have disposed of my obligation. Do you want to settle it, or mulishly fail to, elsewhere?"

Wragg looked at Cramer. "Do you see anything wrong with it?"

The eyes of the cop and the G-man met and held. "No," Cramer said. "Do you?"

"No. You have the gun?"

"Yes." Cramer turned to Wolfe. "You said I might not ask Goodwin after we finished with Wragg. I won't. I may later if we hit a snag. I would only get a run-around, and to hell with it." He went back to Wragg. "It's up to you."

Wragg's hand went to a pocket and came out with a little plastic vial. He rose and took a step. "This bullet," he said, "was found on the floor of Morris Althaus's apartment, in the living room, around eleven o'clock in the evening on Friday, November twentieth. Now it's yours. I have never seen it."

Cramer stood up to take it. He removed the lid of the vial, let the bullet drop into his palm, inspected it, and returned it to the vial.

"You're damned right it's mine," he said.

15

Three evenings later, Monday around half past six, Wolfe and I were in the office, debating a point about the itemization of expenses to go with the bill to Mrs. Bruner. I admit it was a minor point, but it was a matter of principle. He was maintaining that it was just and proper to include the lunch at Rusterman's, on the ground that the meals we got there were in consideration of services he had rendered and was still rendering to the restaurant and so were not actually gratis. My position was that the past services had already been rendered, and the present ones would be rendered, even if she and I had gone to the Automat for lunch.

"I realize," I said, "that you're up against it. Even if you push the fee to the limit, say another hundred grand, it still might not be enough to last the whole year, and around Labor Day, or at least Thanksgiving, you might have to take on a job, so you need to squeeze out every nickel you can. But she has been a marvelous client, and you should have some consideration for her, and indirectly for me too in case I decide to marry her. She has a lot of other expenses besides you, and now she'll have another one, now that she's going to supply a high-priced lawyer to defend Sarah Dacos. Have a heart."

"As you know, Miss Dacos has confessed."

"So she'll need a lawyer even more. I feel very strongly about this. I invited her to lunch. I am almost prepared to say that if she is billed for it I will feel that I must tell her privately that it was on the house. She may want—"

The doorbell rang. I got up and went to the hall and saw a character on the stoop I had never seen before, but I had seen plenty of pictures of him. I stepped back in and said, "Well, well. The *big* fish."

He frowned at me, then got it, and did something he never does. He left his chair and came. We stood side by side, looking. The caller put a finger to the button, and the doorbell rang.

"No appointment," I said. "Shall I take him to the front room to wait a while?"

"No. I have nothing for him. Let him get a sore finger." He turned and went back in to his desk.

I stepped in. "He probably came all the way from Washington just to see you. Quite an honor."

"Pfui. Come and finish this."

I returned to my chair. "As I was saying, I may have to tell her privately . . ."

The doorbell rang.